January 1998

Dear Reader,

Here at Knopf Paperbacks, we're getting ready to celebrate. After all, our first birthday is fast approaching and—as I write this—there are already *forty-eight* Knopf Paperbacks in print. That's four books for every month, one for every week, a chapter for every day...well, you get the picture. It's been a busy first year.

And from the looks of our 1998 lineup, we're about to get busier. This Knopf Paperback Sampler offers a sneak peek at the year to come, with excerpts from twelve of our top novels. And though you might be tempted to flip right to some familiar favorites (Philip Pullman, Dick King-Smith, and Ann Cameron, to name a few), please be sure to turn back and read them all—especially Knopf Paperback newcomers Paul Many, Wendelin Van Draanen, and Elvira Woodruff. I know you'll be glad you did.

In fact, I bet you'll find at least one book here (and maybe two or three...) that will rise right to the top of your "Must Read" list or—better yet!—send you straight out the door to your local bookstore. I'll sign off now and let you find out for yourself.

I hope you enjoy these selections.

All the best,

Joan Slattery
Executive Editor
Knopf Paperbacks

KNOPF PAPERBACKS

A Fiction Sampler • 1998

CONTENTS

ELVIRA WOODRUFF came to write *Dear Levi* after reading the diaries and letters of pioneers who crossed the country in covered wagons in the mid-1800s. A former children's librarian and professional storyteller, she has written more than a dozen picture books and novels for children, including *Dear Napoleon, I Know You're Dead, But...*; *George Washington's Socks*; and *The Orphan of Ellis Island*. *Dear Austin*, the sequel to *Dear Levi*, will be published by Knopf in Fall 1998.

She lives in Martins Creek, Pennsylvania, with her two sons, Noah and Jess.

PRAISE FOR *DEAR LEVI*:

"Filled with hazardous escapades that keep the adrenaline pumping...the epistolary format and character development offer solid reading."

—*Booklist*

"Woodruff presents a bounty of information in a format that will be especially valued as a classroom read-aloud."

—*The Bulletin of the Center for Children's Books*

"Readers will enjoy the details of Austin's developing friendship with two other young boys and his awe and respect for the wise and well-traveled cook, Reuben."

—*The Horn Book*

An IRA Teachers' Choice
A 1999 Virginia Young Readers Award Nominee

from

DEAR LEVI
LETTERS FROM THE OVERLAND TRAIL
by ELVIRA WOODRUFF

May 12, 1851

Dear Levi,

Mr. Morrison says we're two hundred miles or so from Fort Laramie, and if we keep on as we are, we should be there by the beginning of next month. I wish I could hear from you somehow, Levi. I think about you and hope you're well. Frank's little brother Abraham often tags along with us, and sometimes Frank gets so mad. He says he hates to have him always "nosing around." It makes me a little homesick, thinking about how mad I used to get at you for doing the same thing!

After supper, as the men were sitting around the fire, word came down from the wagons ahead that Indians had been sighted some ten miles away. No one seems to know if they're friendly or not. Mr. Hickman let out a hoot as soon as he heard about them. He bragged that he wasn't going to end his trip without "shootin' me an Injun," and a few of the other men laughed at this.

Mr. Morrison did not laugh. He said that Mr. Hickman had no right to kill anyone, Indian or no. Mr. Hickman did not like the sound of that. His eyes got all bulgy, and the big veins along his neck looked as if they were going to pop. He spit some juice not far from Mr. Morrison's boot and then said, "I don't suppose a coward would know much about killing Injuns."

Everyone got real quiet, and I was afraid for Mr. Morrison, as he is a thin man and not as big as Mr. Hickman. Finally Mr. Yardly, an older man, said that he thought we best be getting to bed, so as to be ready tomorrow for whatever the day might bring. Then he got up and walked over to Mr. Morrison.

"I sure would appreciate it if you'd give me a hand with that splintered wheel tomorrow, Tom," he says. "You know the one I was telling you about. Come on, I'll show which one I mean." Mr. Morrison stood up slowly and looked Mr. Hickman right in the eye. I was holding my breath, wondering what would happen next. But Mr. Hickman looked away, and everyone else started talking again.

Frank's face went all red as he sat beside me, twisting his snakeskin around a twig. He was so embarrassed by his pa's remarks that he lowered his eyes and wouldn't look at anyone. All of a sudden it felt strange to be sitting next to him, and I couldn't think of anything to say. Hiram offered to tell us about the Indians that had attacked their house last spring and how he had fought them off single-handed, but neither of us wanted to hear about it.

I can't help feeling uneasy about all of this, and wonder what will come tomorrow.

Your brother, Austin

• • • • •

May 25, 1851

Dear Levi,

We traveled twelve miles today and there was no sign of Indians. I think I ate more sand than biscuit for breakfast. The wind blew up clouds of dust and sand so thick a body could get lost in them. By afternoon the winds were so high that the women couldn't even make a fire to cook on. We are still in Nebraska Territory, camped on the bank of Loup Fork along the Platte River. We are waiting for our turn to cross. It is very dangerous, as parts of the riverbed are made of quicksand. There is a ferry, and for three dollars they will tow the wagon. Mr. Morrison and I will have to swim the stock, though. I've been getting better at this, as Mr. Morrison gives me lessons whenever he's able and there's water about.

Mr. Morrison spends a good deal of his free time teaching me things and talking to me about farming. He even calls me "son" now and again. I know lots of folks call boys that, but I like hearing it just the same.

Frank says that when we get farther along in the territories, he's aiming to run away. His pa took a hickory switch to him for being late with his chores and then again for spilling a bucket of water. His mother, although never mean to Frank, is stony-faced and never smiles. I told Frank that he's welcome to come live with you and me once we get settled. I don't know how such a nice fellow could have such a mean pa. When Frank tripped and dropped the bucket, he cut his foot on a rock. It pained him to walk with the cut, but that didn't make any difference to Mr. Hickman, who insisted he keep to his work.

After supper Hiram, Frank, and I went looking for some cobwebs to lay over Frank's cut. Hiram says that cobwebs are the best cure for a wound. At first Frank wasn't so sure he wanted cobwebs laid on him, but then Hiram called him a coward and said he'd used cobwebs lots of times to cure his cuts. Hiram went on to say that he didn't think there was much of anything that could scare him, not pirates, or lightning, or even rotting dead bodies.

We were poking through some brush, searching for cobwebs, with Hiram still going on about all he wasn't a-scared of, when we came upon a den of prairie dogs. They gave out some yelps, but that was nothing compared to Hiram's scream when a jack rabbit popped up and jumped clear over his head! We never did get those cobwebs, but Frank says he laughed so hard to hear Hiram holler that his cut feels much improved.

Your brother, Austin

• • • • •

June 2, 1851

Dear Levi,

I wish I never lived to see what I had to see today. And there's no telling what will come because of it tomorrow. It all started last night with a terrible storm. The wind in this territory can be very fierce, so fierce it pulled off the Yardlys' wagon cover, and the rain was coming down so hard that everything was soaked through within an hour.

When morning finally came, two oxen were found killed by lightning, and most of the cattle had scattered. Hiram, Frank, and I spent a long time searching for them and herding them back to camp. The going was awfully slow, as it rained on and off and we were in mud up to our hubs. Everyone was worn out from being awake most of the night and feeling cold and soaked through. I was walking with Frank beside his wagon when word suddenly came down that there were Indians up ahead.

On hearing this, Mr. Hickman climbed up into his wagon and came back down with his rifle.

"They didn't say whether they were friendly or not," I whispered to Frank.

"Don't make no difference to my pa," Frank said. "He's been wanting to kill himself an Injun ever since we started this trip."

I wondered what these Indians would be like and if they would put up a good fight against Mr. Hickman and his rifle. I supposed they would have only their bows and arrows, though maybe they'd have poison arrows and tomahawks, too.

We quickened our pace, as everyone was anxious to set eyes on the Indians. When they finally arrived, they were in small groups. They did not look as if they wanted to fight, for there were women among them, and the men were not aiming their arrows. They were offering berries, beads, and moccasins for trade. Some of their women traded berries for bread, and Mr. Taylor traded a lot of hard crackers for a pair of moccasins from a tall, proud-looking Indian man. But after we had started on, the Indian came running back up to Mr. Taylor's wagon, making a fuss and pointing to the moccasins he had traded. Mr. Taylor would not give them back, as the Indian had already eaten some of the crackers. It was clear the Indian did not understand that the crackers were all Mr. Taylor was willing to give for the moccasins.

I was glad to see Reuben slow his wagon to a stop and proceed to get down. I knew he would try and sort things out between the two, but before Reuben could reach their wagon, Mr. Hickman had come around with his rifle. He yelled for the Indian to be off, but the Indian wouldn't budge, except to reach out to take the moccasins back. That's when Mr. Hickman took aim and was about to shoot—just as one of the Indian women stepped into the fray. She was trying to give back the bread when the shot rang out. I saw her drop down into the grass beside the wagon as the smell of gunshot filled my nostrils.

The other Indians all scattered, except for one. The sack of crackers fell from his hands as he knelt down beside the woman. When he knew that she was dead, he flung his head back and cried out. His cry was so sharp and long it was as if all other sounds in the world suddenly died and there was only this one long cry.

Mr. Hart and Reuben had come up by this time and taken the rifle away from Mr. Hickman, having to fight him to the ground for it. Meanwhile, as we all stood watching, the Indian leaning over the dead woman suddenly lifted something up out of the grass, and we were all amazed to see that he was holding a baby! It was so tiny, and had been wrapped so tightly in a sling on the woman's back, that I hadn't even taken notice of it before.

When Mr. Hart and Mr. Morrison tried to approach the Indian, he turned with the baby and ran out of sight. Frank, Hiram, and I waited by the wagons, looking down at the dead Indian woman. She was wearing a white bark dress and moccasins. A leather sling hung empty from her shoulders.

We heard that this young Sioux family had been peacefully trading for hardtack and corn from the party up ahead. Poor Frank couldn't take his eyes off the dead woman, until Mrs. Morrison and some of the others finally covered her with a blanket.

I'd rather have no pa than one who could do such a thing as what Mr. Hickman has done today. "Cold-blooded murder" is what Mr. Morrison called it. Mr. Hickman denied it, saying he was defending our train and that the Indian was preparing to fight. I don't think anyone believed him. But there was no way to prove it. And the strange thing is, even after seeing what he'd done, Mr. Hickman showed no sign of remorse.

"It was just an Injun, just a squaw," he kept muttering. Mr. Morrison was shaking with anger. He believes that all people are God's children. Reuben said that Mr. Hickman should be made to "stretch the rope" for what he done. And Mr. Hart was worried. He ordered a meeting of all the men. He said that we had to prepare ourselves in case the Indians decided to take revenge.

Tonight Mr. Morrison and I are on guard duty. Most of the train is sleeping under their wagons. I have my rifle loaded, and it's here by the fire with me as I write you. I was wondering how I'd find the courage to keep steady if we came under attack, and then I thought about you. You're my only kin, Levi. With Ma and Pa gone, we've nothing left in this world but each other. So I will do what I must to keep alive for you and for us.

It is good to be around someone like Mr. Morrison. He's not a big man, but he's strong in his beliefs and conducts himself in such a manner as to warrant respect. I hope to be like him when I'm grown. I didn't tell him how uneasy I was feeling, but I suspect Mr. Morrison knew, for as we sat together by the fire he told me how he had been afraid at times when he was growing up. Somehow it helped to hear how toads used to give him a fright when he was a small boy.

I can't help thinking about that Indian woman. Hiram figures she might have been an Indian princess, and when we asked Reuben he said we'd better pray she wasn't. She did look as if she could have been a princess, with long black hair and necklaces of beads and feathers around her neck. She seemed very young. I wonder what her life must have been like and how her baby is doing without her. The night is full of critters calling to one another in the darkness, and yet I keep hearing again and again in my mind that long, painful cry.

Your brother, Austin

DICK KING-SMITH was born and raised in Gloucestershire, England. After twenty years as a farmer, he turned to teaching and then to writing the children's books that have earned him critical acclaim on both sides of the Atlantic. Mr. King-Smith is the author of numerous books for children, including *Mr. Ape*, *Martin's Mice*, and *Babe: The Gallant Pig*, which was made into an award-winning major motion picture.

He lives in a seventeenth-century cottage near Bristol, England.

PRAISE FOR *THE STRAY*:

"Full of gentle humor and likable characters . . . The large print and accessible style will make this book popular with independent readers."

—*School Library Journal*

"A sunny story of family and friendship in which good things come to Good people."

—*Kirkus Reviews*

"This cozy, old-fashioned novel...will endear itself to readers in search of big-hearted diversion."

—*Publishers Weekly*

"King-Smith pens a moving tale of kindness, compassion, and families . . . This is a warm and cozy treat, illustrated with delightful art, for independent readers or to share with your youngsters as a family read-aloud."

—*Children's Book Review*

A Bank Street College "Children's Book of the Year"

from

The Stray

by DICK KING-SMITH

Henny had grown used to the occasional sounds of Saltmouth's late night traffic passing Ivy Cottage, but the sound that woke her later was an unusual one. It was a kind of scraping sound, of metal on metal, and it seemed to be coming from beneath her window.

Henny got out of bed, went quietly across the room, and looked out. Directly below was a man who seemed to be trying to open the garage door.

Her first thought was that it was George. But why would he want to get the car out at—she looked at her watch—two o'clock in the morning?

She leaned out a little farther and now could see by the light of the streetlight that it was certainly not George.

George was big. This man was smallish.

George was balding. This man had a lot of hair tied in a ponytail.

George had a key to his garage. This man, she could see, had some sort of crowbar in his hand with which he was trying, as quietly as he could, to force open the garage door.

Some old ladies in Henny's position would have screamed or shouted for help, but all Henny felt was anger, anger on behalf of the Good family, her family, as she already felt them to be.

This nasty thief was actually trying to break in and steal their car, their beautiful big shining eight-seater monster (she had had a ride in it and knew that it would take seven Goods and one Hickathrift).

What's more, he was trying to steal it right under her nose!

If I give a shout for George, she thought, the man will just run away. And I can't very well sneak down the stairs in my blue flannel nightgown with the pattern of red roses and grab him in a headlock. He may be small, but I'm smaller and a heck of a lot older. Besides, he'd most likely knock my teeth out—the ones that aren't in the tooth glass, I mean. What shall I do?

Then her eye fell on Barney's painting of the bomber and then on the money plant at her elbow.

Quickly she picked up the heavy pot and held it out past the window sill.

Carefully, though her arms began to ache with the weight of it, she moved the pot a fraction this way and that—just like a bombsight in an airplane—till it was, she judged, directly above that ponytailed head below.

Then she dropped it.

■ ■ ■ ■ ■

At breakfast the next morning the children were told all about the bombing of the burglar.

"I was woken up by the sound of Henny shouting my name," their father said, "and when I got outside, there was this chap knocked out cold. I recognized him straightaway, because he was lying on his back with his mouth open, and when I shone the flashlight on him I could see the repair work I'd done on his upper left four. It was young Freddie Hooper—Hooper the boatman's oldest boy."

"The one with the ponytail, Dad?" asked Barney.

"Yes. He's been in trouble with the police before now."

"Are you going to report him?" asked Angela.

"No. I don't think he'll try breaking into our garage again. He was so dazed he had no idea what had happened. I told him it was part of our security system. Anyway, there wasn't any damage to the door worth speaking of, only to his head. He had a bump on it the size of a hen's egg."

"Oh, dear!" said Henny. "And I broke your flowerpot too, Mary."

"Don't worry," said Mary. "I've got loads of pots and lots more money plants. I'll give you another one for your room, and then we won't ever need to worry about having the car stolen, thanks to the Patented Hickathrift Antiburglar Bomb."

"We're very grateful to Henny," George said to the rest. "Aren't we?" Everyone cried, "Yes!" and then they all clapped and then they sang "For She's a Jolly Good Fellow!"

Henny looked at the five red-haired children and their tall fair-haired mother and their big balding father and thought what jolly Good fellows *they* all were.

After breakfast, when the dentist had left for his office and the children for school—for the new term had started—Mary said, "Well, Henny, the month is up."

"What month?" said Henny.

"Your trial month. Remember, we agreed to give it a try to see how it worked out?"

"Oh, yes," said Henny.

Oh, no, she thought. Don't tell me she's going to say I've got to go! I couldn't bear to be a stray again.

"Well, what d'you think?" said Mary.

"Think?"

"I mean, is the work too much for you?"

"Oh, no!"

"Are you happy with us?"

"Oh, yes!"

"Well, it's all right, then," said Mary.

"I can stay?" said Henny.

"Couldn't manage without you. Did I tell you I've signed up for a college course? In French. We go to France quite often on vacation, so it'll be useful. I hardly took any French when I was in school, and George took none—he just shouts at them slowly in English. Which reminds me, I must get myself a French dictionary. Oh, and I must go and find you another money plant."

"Speaking of money," Henny said. "I haven't given you any, you know. I must pay for my bed and board. We agreed I should."

"Don't worry about that," said Mary. "You more than earn your keep with all the work you do. By the way, could you do a bit of shopping for me this morning? Nothing heavy."

In the town Henny collected the few little things on Mary's list. One of them was a lottery ticket, and just for luck Henny got one for herself as well. Then she treated herself to a box of jujubes.

As she sucked one of these, held between her new teeth, she had a brainstorm. I've got quite a lot of money now, she thought, because Mary won't take any. But she can't stop me from buying her a present. And she made her way to a bookshop.

"Just look at this!" said Mary Good to her husband when he came home for lunch, and she put before him a very large new dictionary, on whose shiny cover was written:

FRENCH–ENGLISH

ANGLAIS–FRANÇAIS

George picked it up, looked at the price on it, and gave a whistle.

"Twenty quid!" he said. "You've gone all out!"

"Look inside," said his wife.

On the flyleaf was written:

TO MARY GOOD

FROM HENRIETTA HICKATHRIFT

Henny came into the room.

"How very generous of you, Henny," said George, brandishing the heavy book.

"It's you two that are generous to me," said Henny. "I only wish there was some way I could repay you for your kindness."

Perhaps I could win some money with this thing, she thought later. She was sitting on a chair outside Ivy Cottage, her lottery ticket in her lap, watching the evening sun on the sea. I wonder what you have to do? The children will know.

The children were playing croquet on the lawn. It was a very special and difficult sort of croquet, because the slope meant that the croquet balls all tended to roll down toward the sea wall, and anyway, that's where the players tried to knock one another. It was also a dangerous game, as Henny had found out on the one and only occasion on which she had played, because everyone hit the croquet balls as hard as they could and your ankles were in great danger.

When the game was finished, four of them came up the lawn toward her, red heads bright in the evening sun.

Barney was grinning because he had won.

Angela was smiling because she didn't mind not having won.

Eleanor and Rosie were quite happy because they never won anyway.

Behind them Rowley was still playing all by himself. He placed the ball right in front of each hoop and then knocked it through, the only way he ever scored anything.

"Tell me," said Henny to the four older ones. "Do you know how to do this lottery thing?"

"I do," said Angela. "I've seen Mom do it. You have to

choose six numbers between one and forty-nine. That costs you a pound. Then when it comes to the draw, if you've got the first five numbers that they call out, you can win an awful lot of money."

Rowley arrived in time to hear this.

"Seventy million pounds," he said. "A man did."

"Seven*teen* million," the others said.

"I don't think I'd want to win that much," Henny said. "I wouldn't know what to do with it."

"Give it to us," said Rowley.

"I have to choose six, did you say?" asked Henny.

"Yes."

"Well, look, there's me and there's the five of you. Let's each pick a number. Start with the youngest. What number d'you want, Rowley?"

"Five," said Rowley. "Because that's what I'm going to be, soon."

Then the rest made a choice, in turn, and each time Henny made against the chosen number a clean vertical line with a ballpoint pen, as the instructions said.

"There we are, then," she said at last. "Five, twenty-five, thirty-one, thirty-nine, forty-four."

"Six," said Angela. "You have to pick six numbers, Henny. What are you going to pick?"

"Oh, I don't know. Let's see, I'll say thirteen."

"That's unlucky," said Rowley.

"Which is what I shall be, Rowley, you can bet your bottom dollar," said Henny. "I never win these sorts of things. Waste of a pound, really."

MONICA FURLONG is the author of several noteworthy biographies of prominent spiritual figures, including Thomas Merton, Alan Watts, and Saint Thérèse de Lisieux, as well as the best-selling young adult novels *Wise Child* and *Juniper*.

She lives in London, England.

PRAISE FOR *ROBIN'S COUNTRY*:

"Furlong's prose beautifully and magically evokes the medieval forest setting."

—School Library Journal

"Filled with adventure and swagger that will attract readers."

—Booklist

"Readers who find Sherwood irresistible will appreciate a chance to romp through the forest."

—The Bulletin of the Center for Children's Books

"A lively version of the Robin Hood legend."

—Children's Book Review

A Bank Street College "Children's Book of the Year"

A 1998 Young Readers Choice Award Nominee (Pacific Northwest)

ROBIN'S COUNTRY

from

ROBIN'S COUNTRY

by MONICA FURLONG

The next day was one Dummy never forgot. He was in a deep sleep when he heard Robin whisper, "Come with me, Bird. We have work to do." He longed to go on sleeping, but he knew he must obey Robin's command, and in a few moments he was out of his warm bed, pulling on his breeches, and splashing cold water on his face.

When he joined Robin outside, Dummy scarcely recognized him. Robin was not wearing his short tunic of Lincoln green over dark green hose, with shoes and hood of green-dyed leather. Instead he wore the long serge robe of a monk, a patched white garment with a cowl. He had sandals upon his bare feet. Dummy could not conceal his surprise.

"A shock, eh, Bird?" laughed Robin. "This is a day for a good disguise."

The two of them set off on the long walk to Nottingham, though a kindly farmer took them part of the way in his cart. It was midday before they reached the city, and they were both thirsty. As they turned in at an alehouse, Robin, Dummy noticed, no longer walked with the long stride of the hunter but with the slow, short step of man accustomed to pace a cloister, reading as he walked. They sat on a bench by a filthy, stained table. With the timid gesture of one unused to the world, Robin called to the landlord in a high, reedy voice.

The landlord tried to ignore him at first. "I don't want no monks begging in here, Joan," he muttered to his wife. "Let me have customers who can pay for their drink."

"I have money," Robin answered. He took out a coin and laid it on the table in front of him. Joan came to serve him.

"Don't pay no attention to him, Father," she said. "Me, I'm glad enough to have a holy gentleman like yourself in here— it's a privilege. What brings you out of the cloister to this god-forsaken place?"

"No place is without God's love," said Robin piously. "I am come to Nottingham to fetch this lad, a novice who is joining the Abbey of Rievaulx."

"You are come a long way, Father, for such a scrap of a lad."

"We need to quench our thirst before we travel on," said Robin, "and to find out what local news there is to take back to my brethren at Rievaulx."

"News?" said Joan, wiping the perspiration off her face with the end of her long sleeve and turning to her husband. "Have we any news, Master Gregory?"

The landlord thought for a moment. "There's a hanging this afternoon," he said. "Laborer Tom caught red-handed shooting a deer. I might go along to watch that."

"I'm glad to hear it," said Robin righteously. "Venison is not fit meat for peasants, and all should know it."

"I did hear that he's got small children at home and nothing to feed them on," said Joan, pity in her voice.

"Stealing is a grave sin," said Robin, shaking his head. "And doubly wrong when it is thieving the king's property."

"But when people are hungry," Joan said doubtfully, "and all those great fat deer wander about in the Forest . . ."

"Landlord," said Robin sharply. "Your wife's tongue is running away with her. She will be talking treason next."

"Be quiet, Mistress," said the landlord, looking anxious.

"Any more news?" asked Robin.

"There's the shooting match at Corpus Christi," said the landlord, more respectful of his customer since the mention of treason. "Sheriff organized it. Men are coming from all over to take part. But that wouldn't interest a man like yourself."

"It would interest my brothers back in the cloister," Robin said. "They love to hear how the world goes. What is the prize?"

"An arrow of the purest beaten gold," said the landlord. "Our sheriff does things handsomely when he's a mind."

"He wastes our taxes," Joan grumbled to herself, but her husband, who clearly liked the thought of the contest, paid no attention to her.

They left the alehouse and Robin walked on, with a slow, stumbling gait that Dummy found hard to match, to the Sheriff of Nottingham's house, pausing only at a butcher's shop in the public square where Robin conferred with the shopkeeper. Dummy watched fascinated as a big wooden scaffold, a platform with a gibbet on the top, was erected in the middle of the square. On the far side of the scaffold stood the magnificent house that belonged to the Sheriff. It was so big that it took up one whole side of the square, its black and white timbers hanging over the street. By chance the Sheriff himself stood on the doorstep, talking to a departing guest. He wore a fine crimson robe, trimmed with fur, over his full belly. His broad crimson hat matched the color of his cheeks.

Robin stood beside the steps, head meekly bowed beneath his cowl, arms tucked in his long sleeves.

"Sir," he began, in a high, timid voice. The Sheriff, who was calling a witticism after his guests, ignored him.

"Sir!" Robin said again, as the Sheriff turned. The Sheriff paused for a moment, one foot on the threshold, and looked at him.

"I am offering myself as confessor," Robin said. "For the man who is to be hanged this afternoon."

"Do you know him?" the Sheriff asked crossly.

"I am passing through this town, and heard of his fate. It seemed to me that God has called me to minister to this poor man."

"He richly deserves to die."

"Of course. But a pious, God-fearing man such as yourself would not wish to refuse him absolution before he dies. And I shall instruct him to pray for you in his last prayers."

Dummy knew, because Robin had told him, that only the year before a man who was hanged had publicly cursed the Sheriff with his dying breath, and the very next day the Sheriff's favorite horse had sickened and died. The story of this, and also of the Sheriff's superstitious fear, had been all over town.

"Very well," said the Sheriff. "It can do no harm."

"And shall I get paid for my service?" asked Robin.

"I thought God had called you to perform it," said the Sheriff sharply. "Is not that payment enough?"

"A poor monk must live, sir," Robin replied meekly.

"Must drink, you probably mean," said the Sheriff contemptuously, but he pulled a silver coin out of his pocket and threw it at Robin so that it fell on the pavement and Robin had to scramble for it in the gutter. The Sheriff laughed, went into his house, and shut the door.

"Do you know the way from here to the blasted oak?" Robin suddenly asked Dummy. "The hollow oak by the track we passed as we came out of the Forest this morning?"

Dummy had a good sense of direction and he nodded eagerly.

"Leave me for a while," said Robin. "But stay near me in the crowd this afternoon and watch what happens. When it's all over I will meet you by the oak." He gave Dummy money to buy bread and cheese, turned on his heel, and disappeared in the direction of the town jail.

That afternoon Dummy watched as Robin walked with the criminal, Tom, through the streets of Nottingham. When men were executed they were first heavily beaten at the jail, then tied to a shutter and dragged through the streets at the tail of a cart. On the scaffold itself they were strung up to be hanged, then, before they were quite dead, they were cut down and disemboweled. It was a terrible death.

As the procession wound through the streets from the jail, citizens lined the route, fascinated at the sight of the pale criminal, already covered in blood, his eyes rolling in his head with terror, his head bumping along in the dirt and dust of the road. Dummy heard him muttering prayers to Mary and to Jesus, occasionally calling out the names of his wife and children.

Robin paced slowly behind him, intoning pious sentences out loud. "Think upon your sins, which are many. Let this be a sign to all who are tempted to wrongdoing. We shall see justice done this day."

Once or twice he bent down and lifted Tom's head, holding it out of the mire, and he seemed to be conferring with him. Dummy wondered what he could be saying. When they reached the public square the drums began to beat more insistently, and the executioner waited on the platform beneath the gibbet with several assistants beside him. At the Sheriff's house one of the casements of an upstairs window had been removed, and the Sheriff and his wife stood at the window waiting to see justice done. Tom staggered so much when they untied him from the shutter that he could scarcely walk, and Robin was obliged to help him to his feet, which he did coldly and unsympathetically. The executioner bade them mount the scaffold, but Robin demurred.

"I must hear this man's confession in a private place," he announced. "I must grant him time to say prayers of penance, including a prayer for Sir Sheriff. If the butcher will grant us the use of his shop for a few minutes, this will be quickly accomplished."

The executioner looked up at the Sheriff for permission. The square was full of people who would be shocked if the monk's plea was refused. The Sheriff nodded at the executioner, and the monk helped the half-fainting man into the butcher's shop and shut the door.

As the sun shone brightly down on the public square, the crowd speculated about what sins Tom was confessing.

"Please, Father, I stole a kiss from Betsy Watkins," one onlooker shouted out.

"Oh, my son, that is very wicked, even worse than stealing a deer," cried another.

"I nicked a purse from the Sheriff's servant."

"A thousand Hail Marys for you!"

Dummy could see that the Sheriff suspected he was being

mocked and that he did not like being kept waiting for the execution any more than the crowd did.

"Go and knock on the door," he called to the executioner. "Tell them to hurry up."

The executioner did as he was told, and the crowd waited for another few minutes. Finally, at a nod from the Sheriff, the executioner tried to open the door, only to find that it was locked from within. He banged and rattled at it, but it did not open. Finally, using his strong shoulder, he forced the lock and disappeared inside. Almost at once he reappeared with the monk's white robe in his arms and a look of horror on his face.

"They are gone, Sir Sheriff," he stammered. "The shop is empty, and the gate into the lane at the back hangs open."

The Sheriff stared down at him unbelievingly.

"There was something else too. Written in blood from the butcher's offal pail there were some words scribbled on the wall."

"What words?" asked the Sheriff.

"'Robin Hood,' my lord."

It took a moment for the Sheriff to recover from his surprise, but then he began shouting orders, orders that could barely be heard over the noise of the crowd. For its mood had changed, Dummy saw. A few minutes before, the crowd had thought only of seeing Tom killed. Now, thanks to Robin's bravery and audacity, they wanted Tom to escape. They laughed scornfully at the expression of outrage on the Sheriff's purple face. Clusters of mocking people gathered at the roads leading out of the square. They jeered at the Sheriff's sergeants, who were trying to set out in search of Tom and Robin. More important, they kept them from leaving. Much time elapsed before the Sheriff's horsemen managed to ride away.

With some difficulty Dummy struggled through the crowds and made his way to the oak tree by the track. At first he could see no sign of Robin, but suddenly there was a merry shout, and Robin swung down from the branches. A moment later Tom's scared face appeared among the leaves.

"That was a good day, Bird," Robin said triumphantly. Dummy noticed that he seemed exhilarated, and had a feeling that danger always made Robin excited. Later, as he picked out a new tune on his pipes, Dummy listened to poor Tom stammering out his gratitude.

"If it wasn't for you I would have been dead these last six hours," he said to Robin. "How can I thank you?"

"One day," said Robin, "we may need our friends to rise up in our defense, but in the meantime, go to your wife and family, now safely far away in Yorkshire, and live in gratitude to God for sparing you." Tom nodded.

Dummy realized that his old master had simply been wrong about Robin Hood, as he had been wrong about many things. Robin was a hero, and, one day, he hoped, he would be just like him.

SALLY WARNER is the author of *Dog Years* and *Some Friends*. Her newest novel, *Sort of Forever*, will be published by Knopf in Spring 1998. An art and education teacher for many years, she now devotes herself full-time to drawing and writing. Ms. Warner has two grown sons, one of whom is a dancer with the Pittsburgh Ballet.

She makes her home in Pasadena, California.

from

Ellie & the Bunheads

by SALLY WARNER

Middle school is really all about hair, and I can prove it. If you are having a bad hair day, you might as well stay home. The world will turn on you. Nothing will go right—classes, tests, nothing. Even lunch. But if your hair is looking good, you have a chance. Luckily, my hair is just about my best feature. And that fact is probably the main reason I'm doing okay at school. Advance self-improvement: Keep it looking good. Shampoo at least every other day, always use conditioner, use a comb for tangles, use a brush for shine.

—To be continued.

ELLIE & THE BUNHEADS

"That's not what you're going to wear, is it?" her mother asked late that Sunday afternoon. Dr. Amory was picking Ellie up at five, in only half an hour.

"Bella *said* it was casual," Ellie replied, trying not to look at herself in the mirror while her mother was still in the room. Why give her the satisfaction? "Their Sunday dinners always are."

"Well, casual's one thing, but . . ." Mrs. Lane's worried voice trailed off, and the room was silent for a moment.

"Jeans and a sweater is casual, Mom," Ellie said. "There are no holes, and everything's clean—including my hair, you'll be glad to hear." Her mom never had to remind Ellie about washing her hair, but she always did anyway.

"Your hair looks nice, darling," her mother said, sounding as though she was eager to compliment her daughter on *something*.

It was true, though. Ellie's hair was a medium brown, which sounded ordinary. But it never looked boring; it was shiny and smooth, even when she was a bunhead. When she wore her hair down, which was all the time she wasn't dancing, its heaviness—which was emphasized by a straight cut kept perfect at her mom's beauty salon—made it her strongest point, Ellie secretly felt. Her eyes weren't too bad either.

Sometimes Ellie looked at herself in the mirror and tried to figure out why she looked the way she did. Where did a person's looks come from?

Her hair? It looked like her mother's, when her mom had been a little girl. Now, her mom's hair was permed and frosted; it was hard to tell *what* color it was anymore. Ellie promised herself she would never do that to her own hair.

Her green eyes? They were like her father's, though the gold flecks were more like her grandma's. Her oval face with its pointed chin was definitely her grandma's. The dimple came from her mom, probably.

Ellie's long legs came from her dad. Probably her shoulders did too, she thought gloomily. Her shoulders were too wide.

She wondered sometimes if any part of the way she looked was just hers. Her skin maybe; she always tried to keep it clean. Perhaps her figure was hers too. She was careful about what she ate—most of the time, anyway, and with her mother's nagging. Anyway, her posture was definitely hers. Well, hers and Ms. Hawkins's.

Ellie had finally decided that maybe you were born a certain way, but after that, what you did with it was up to you—more and more so every year. She hoped so, anyway. Ellie grimaced guiltily as she pictured her mother's bulges and her father's tired slump. Someday she would be a person separate from her parents and all their problems!

"Ellie?" her mother was saying. "Are you listening to me?"

"Sorry," Ellie said. "What?"

"Sweetie, I was saying that sweater's okay, but if I can't persuade you to change your pants, won't you at least change your shoes? You have those nice new ones."

"My sneakers are fine, Mom," Ellie said.

Her mother sighed, then changed the subject. "Now don't go eating everything in sight when you're there," she said, "but be sure at least to taste everything at least once."

"Okay," Ellie said. "I can always spit it out on the table-cloth if I don't like it."

"Ellie, for heaven's sake!"

"Look, give me a break," Ellie said, her patience gone. "It's just a meal, Mom. It's only food. You're always making fun of Bella—what do you care whether I behave like a yahoo at her house or not?"

"Ellie, I don't make fun of Arabella Amory. That's not fair. And I *do* care what others think of you—I admit it! I'm your mother, after all."

"What does that have to do with anything, Mom?"

"Plenty."

"But I'm almost thirteen! The way I dress isn't any reflection on *you.*"

"Yes it is, and the way you behave is, too."

Ellie narrowed her eyes and tried to control her temper. "What about the way I dance, Mom?" she blurted out. "Is that *you* too? And—and what about the way you and Daddy act around each other? Is that supposed to be all my fault?"

Ellie's mother looked astonished. She opened her mouth to speak, but then the doorbell rang. Bella was at the door, Dr. Amory was waiting double-parked on Pine Street, and it was time to go.

The Amorys lived on Delancey Street, in the Society Hill section of Philadelphia. Their house wasn't all that far from Mr. Lane's market. Ellie wondered if Mrs. Amory ever shopped there—but she couldn't picture it.

Ellie used to think that Society Hill was named for all the rich people who lived there, but she knew now that—like many areas of Philadelphia—the district was a social patchwork. She also knew that "Society" didn't mean snobs, in this case. It wasn't short for the Society of Friends, either, which was another way of saying Quaker, although Quakers had played an important part in the city's history. No, the Society Hill section had been named for the trading society that had been powerful in the area more than three hundred years ago.

There was really nothing to be nervous about, Ellie knew, but as she climbed into the waiting car, she felt as though she were stepping into a submarine to visit some foreign environment—a happy family, maybe. Oh, why had she said those things to her mom?

"Ellie?" Bella was saying. "This is my dad."

"Hi, Ellie," the man in the driver's seat said, turning awkwardly around.

"How do you do, Dr. Amory," Ellie said. She had been coached by her mother. Bella's father didn't look like Ellie's idea of a doctor, though; he looked as though he had been out hiking, or something.

"Heard a lot about you, from Bella. Glad you could come," he said, his voice cheerful.

"Oh, thanks," Ellie said, but Bella's father had turned his concentration back to driving.

"It's only chili for dinner tonight. I hope that's okay," Bella said softly.

"I love chili," Ellie said.

"My mom makes it with chicken—it's good. She made some corn bread, too, and a salad."

Ellie's stomach gurgled, and she hoped no one could hear it. Mrs. Amory cooked dinner, she thought, surprised. She had imagined that the tall blond woman she'd seen watching class occasionally—the woman whose hair was never mussed, whose clothes were always perfect—would have servants to take care of such things. Ellie felt both relieved and disappointed.

"We got lucky—there's a parking spot," Dr. Amory said, pulling up in front of a rosy brick house with black shutters and a fancy black iron fence in front. This part of the city was so old that very few houses had driveways. Dr. Amory probably drove his car each night to a nearby parking garage, Ellie decided.

The rooms inside the big house were mostly hidden from

view by sheer gathered curtains. Ellie waited as Bella's father fumbled with his key, and she suddenly wished she had worn the new shoes instead of her sneakers. Well, she would have, if her mother hadn't come barging in! What would Mrs. Amory think?

"Ellie! We're so glad you could come," Bella's mother said, swinging open the big front door. She gave her husband a little kiss on his cheek. "Ready in ten minutes, Peter," she said. "And your beeper went off while you were out."

"Oh, no, I forgot it again," he said, patting at his waist.

"Don't worry, you always have Bella and me to look out for you," Mrs. Amory said playfully, winking at Ellie. "Listen, darling," she said to her husband, "why don't you go call the exchange? The girls can wash up and then help me set the table. They'll have plenty of time to visit after supper."

Ellie sneaked curious looks around her as she and Bella carried plates to the dining room. Instead of everything being either all very old or all entirely new, as she had imagined, the Amorys' rooms were a mixture of old and new furniture, old and new lamps. The pictures all looked old, though. Everything was very clean, and there was practically no mess, Ellie noticed, thinking of her own cluttered home.

She felt a sudden unexpected pang of sympathy for her mother, who was always trying to keep everything in the Lanes' apartment just so. Maybe this was what she had been aiming for. Margot Fonteyn could have moved right in.

To Ellie's surprise, dinner was fun. They served themselves from bright ceramic bowls set out on a side table, and they talked and laughed throughout the meal. Dr. Amory liked to joke, and he and his wife even looked as if they were flirting at times. That would be so weird, Ellie thought, trying to imagine her own parents doing the same.

"Bella, elbows," Mrs. Amory said once.

Once was all it took. Bella removed her offending elbow from the table and straightened her spine before her mother could correct her posture. Ellie sat up straighter too. "I've seen you in class, dear," Mrs. Amory said, beaming a bright smile at her. "You're very good."

"Thank you," Ellie said, embarrassed.

"You must be terrific," Dr. Amory observed. "My wife doesn't hand out compliments lightly."

Ellie looked at him, unsure of how to react. Was he complaining about Mrs. Amory?

"Is there any more chili?" Bella asked.

"I think you've had enough, darling," her mother said gently.

"But I'm still hungry," Bella objected.

"There's some left," her father said, lifting the lid and peering into the bowl.

"Then help yourself," Mrs. Amory said smoothly, smiling at Ellie. "More salad, Bella? Ellie?"

When her mom wasn't looking, Bella made a face at Ellie.

Boy, Ellie thought. Her own mom would probably have dragged the bathroom scales into the dining room by now to make her point.

"We'll go out for dessert if you girls are hungry later," Dr. Amory said, as if reassuring his daughter and her friend. "How does a frozen yogurt extravaganza sound?"

"Great," Ellie and Bella replied together. Mrs. Amory rolled her eyes.

Dr. Amory laughed. "Okay. You kids go on upstairs for a while—we'll leave here at eight-thirty. I'll take care of the dishes."

"Thanks, Daddy," Bella said, giving him a hug.

As the two girls climbed the stairs, Ellie slid her hand along the silky wood banister. "I think it's so great that your dad does the dishes," she said.

"Well, they both work," Bella answered with a shrug.

"I didn't know your mother had a job," Ellie said. "I mean, she comes to watch ballet class and everything."

"She only watches class when she can. I wish she *wouldn't.*" Bella was bitter. "Sometimes it feels like she's taking over my life!"

"Yeah, I know what you mean," Ellie said, a little surprised that Bella felt that way too. Mrs. Amory seemed so nice, even when she was saying all her mom stuff. Nice compared to Ellie's mother, anyway. Bella didn't know how lucky she was!

Ellie looked around Bella's bedroom. It was big—it even had a fireplace. And her bed, at least, matched Ellie's fantasies: a lacy canopy arched over it. Ellie imagined waking up in such a bed. Someone, a kindly old housekeeper maybe, would have lit a fire in the fireplace, and . . .

"So listen," Bella was saying, her voice serious. "You've got to help me. That's what I wanted to talk to you about."

Ellie pulled herself away from her daydream. "Why, what's wrong?" she asked, kicking off her sneakers and sitting cross-legged on Bella's big bed.

"I start with that coach tomorrow, after school. You know, getting ready for the audition."

"So you'll have to go to the coach *and* take class?"

Bella nodded. "It's pointe class on Monday. You know we can't miss pointe."

"Oh, yeah," Ellie said. "Well, but what can you do?"

"That's what you've got to help me figure out. I've been thinking like crazy," Bella said.

"What have you come up with so far?"

"Well, I thought about getting sick the day of the audition. But that would never work—my dad's a doctor. You can't fake anything with him."

"That's too bad. What about an injury? Faking it, I mean, not jumping in front of a bus or anything."

"No, they'd just rush me over to Daddy's hospital for x-rays and stuff. Maybe I could arrange a minor injury, though…"

"Bella, you—"

"Oh, not where I break my leg, necessarily. Nothing too drastic. But maybe a twisted ankle? I could always fall down a couple of stairs."

"But twisted ankles *hurt*. You're talking about bruises and swelling. You can't fake that," Ellie objected.

"I'm not talking about faking it."

"You'd really hurl yourself down the staircase?"

"Maybe at school," Bella said, nodding. "They'd freak, so many kids' parents are lawyers!"

Ellie laughed. "Well, let's see what else we can come up with first. How about . . . amnesia?"

"Or abduction," Bella said jokingly. "I could pretend to be kidnapped, and they'd be so relieved to get me back without paying any ransom, they'd forget all about the audition."

"Maybe *I* should try that one," Ellie said.

"Oh, Ellie—were you serious about not wanting to try out?"

"Well, maybe," Ellie admitted slowly. "I'd like to have a choice, at least. My mom acts like it's a given. That's what gets me."

"But you're so good!"

"Bella, if I get in the company, it means I'll be taking class Monday through Friday and then rehearsing all day Saturday. That pretty much rules out anything else, including a social life. Don't you think that should be *my* decision to make?"

"I don't think I'd care, if I could dance like you. My mom says you're a natural."

"Nobody was born doing ballet. We're both at the same level. It's not like you can't—"

"Oh, come on, you know what I mean. There's a difference, Ellie. I could never, ever join a professional company, for one thing."

"Would you want to?"

"I don't know. I'd like to be good enough to be able to,"

Bella admitted. "Like you. Like Dawn, too, for that matter."

"Do you think that's what Dawn wants to do?" Ellie asked. "She keeps saying how terrible she thinks she is, lately."

"You know her better than I do," Bella said, shrugging. "Does she want to keep on dancing? She seems pretty serious to me."

Ellie thought of telling Bella about the dinner Friday night, and about Dawn's problem, but her mom had told her to keep it confidential. "Well," she said instead, "I know what I could do to get out of the audition. Maybe I *will* do it, as a matter of fact."

"What?"

"Oh, maybe I shouldn't tell you. It's pretty radical," Ellie teased.

"*Ellie* . . ."

"Okay," Ellie finally said. "What's the worst thing a bun-head could ever do?"

"I don't know, what?" Bella asked.

"Cut off her . . ."

"Her what?" Bella asked, looking confused.

"Her bun!" Ellie exclaimed. Bella looked as though she couldn't believe what Ellie had said. "Her hair, that's right," Ellie said, nodding. "Just hack the old ballerina bun right off. Save it for Halloween, maybe. Put it on a plate with some Snickers bars and scare the little kids."

"But what good—"

"It's simple, really," Ellie explained. "You know how you

have to wear your hair up once you get past a certain level in dance?" This rule was a firm tradition in the Philadelphia Dance Theater; female ballet dancers couldn't have short hair, because that wasn't traditional. They couldn't have medium-length hair, because it would get in their eyes during turns. No, girl dancers had to wear their hair up in a bun, with no bangs. This led to the "bunhead" nickname Ellie had overheard some male dancers use once; ever since, she hadn't been able to get the word out of her mind.

"You're right," Bella said slowly. "Ms. Hawkins would never make an exception to that company rule, no matter what."

"No," Ellie agreed. "It would be like spitting in the face of all that tradition. And can you imagine Ms. Hawkins spitting?"

Bella grinned at her and shook her head. "Ellie, you're positively brilliant."

"No, I'm not," Ellie said, laughing, "just twisted!"

"Okay, then, *twisted*," Bella agreed. "Now, listen—Daddy loves to treat, so order whatever you want to at the yogurt shop, okay?"

"If you insist," Ellie said.

Though *These Are the Rules* is **PAUL MANY's** first novel, his career is long and varied: street vendor, mail handler, stock boy, janitor, plumber, counselor, waiter, and reporter. He is currently a professor of journalism at the University of Toledo.

He lives with his wife, Linda, and daughter, Zoe, in Ottawa Hills, Ohio.

PRAISE FOR *THESE ARE THE RULES*:

"Laugh-out-loud funny, Many's story is the archetypal YA first-person narrative."

—*Booklist*

"In this debut novel, Many adroitly captures the nuances and ironies of teenage ups and downs with irreverent humor and contemporary dialogue . . . Many is an author to watch."

—*School Library Journal*

"Colm is a likable protagonist in an absorbing plot, and that makes this a winner all around."

—*The Bulletin of the Center for Children's Books*

"A wry account of [a teenager's] trials . . . the narrator's sharp wit will keep the reader tuned into his roller-coaster ride toward adulthood."

—*Publishers Weekly*

"A realistic and absorbing novel."

—*Kirkus Reviews*

from

THESE ARE THE RULES

by PAUL MANY

Next Friday, I was sitting out on the front steps lining up the sights on my BB gun at a soda can across the street, when I caught some movement out of the corner of my eye. It was Carmella, live and in person. She wasn't supposed to come out until the next day, but there she was—tanned and gorgeous in her short shorts, white blouse tied up above her midriff, a big straw bag over her shoulder.

"Come swimming with me," she said. It was part command, part promise, and no part question. I quickly put down the gun. Plinking cans seemed like such a kid thing to be doing. I was speechless.

"You OK?" she said, looking a little worried.

"Sure," I said. "I mean, OK, I'd really like to go with you," and I ran in and got suited up.

I told my mom where I was going and took a quick check in the mirror. One thing, at least with all the swimming, my build wasn't so bad. Although I'd lost a little since I quit over the winter, definition was coming back nice with all the work I was getting in.

"Let's see that Dean guy get pumped like this from spinning a steering wheel," I thought, throwing a towel around my neck.

It was one of those perfect days you get in early summer: not too hot or too cool, a sky made bluer by one bright, backlit cloud, and just enough breeze to push a few strands of hair across Carmella's face where they caught in the corners of her mouth and she slowly drew them out, all wet on the ends. As we walked—it was only a couple of blocks along the lake to the beach—she saw something out in the water—it looked like a heron—and got real close next to me and pointed so I breathed in her perfume.

The beach was deserted. Too early in the morning for anyone to be there except for a few kids and a bored lifeguard who didn't do much guarding for the time it took Carmella to wriggle out of her tight shorts. Underneath, she had on a two-piece, wider than a lot of girls were wearing that year, something her mother probably "helped" her to pick out, and when she took off the blouse, you could see she was still not as tanned on her stomach.

She no sooner kicked her sandals off than she was running. I followed close behind. She dove, expertly slicing into the water, and with quiet strokes was out at the raft in a minute or two. She pulled herself up on it in one smooth move, and when

I tried to get up, she laughed and pushed me back in with her foot. I dove under and came up on the other side of the raft and quickly pulled myself up before she could get me, and tried to wrestle her in, but she was strong and when I shoved harder, she stepped aside and I went flying in.

"Truce. Truce," she said as I grabbed the side of the raft. She put out a hand to help me up, but let go and I fell in again. Next time I grabbed the side and shot myself up out of the water and onto the raft, landing so hard on my stomach that I was winded for a few seconds and lay there like a fish pulled into a boat.

"Colm?" she said, worried, touching my back with the tips of her fingers. I had the taste of tin you get in your mouth when you've gotten a good wallop, but I swallowed it down, and said, "I'm fine."

Fortunately, she lay down next to me so I didn't have to try standing up. It was much warmer out on the raft, and we lay side by side like this in the sun for a while, drying off. She told me about her first couple of weeks working the office job in the city—her first real job after baby-sitting. On her first day of work, an old metal wastebasket had started smoking, right there in the middle of the office, and nobody seemed to notice, so she tried to ignore it too, even though it was right near her desk. Finally, it triggered off the smoke alarm and someone put a fire extinguisher to it.

When they asked her why she didn't say anything, she

said, "I thought that's what you did with your trash." Everyone laughed and she felt embarrassed. "But how would I know? No one told me," she said.

It did sound kind of dumb, but maybe I would've done the same. Who knows? It was like everything else: How do you really know until it happens to you?

"It's hard to figure out what's the right thing to do all the time," I said.

Suddenly, Carmella raised up on an elbow and looked at something on my other side, and I turned to see the familiar, old, beat-up canoe bearing down on us, Marlene leisurely paddling from its stern. What was she doing here? I lay back down like I didn't see her. She came right up to the raft, bumping the canoe into it.

"Hi, Colm. Carmella," she said. "Hi," I said, putting up an arm, but not sitting up. I put the arm over my eyes as if to cover them from the sun. "Long time . . ." This to Carmella. "What're you guys doing out here so early, anyways?"

I mumbled something about "hanging out," then realized what a double meaning it had and got all embarrassed. I felt awkward like I was caught at something I shouldn't be doing. But what? Carmella was very gracious, though, and she and Marlene talked a little while about what they'd done the year before and then Marlene said to me: "Colm, you practicing lately? You haven't been out."

"Practicing for what?" Carmella asked me.

"Colm's trying to swim the lake," said Marlene, beaming like I was her little brother or something.

"Across the *whole* lake?" said Carmella with a little too much show.

"I don't know," I said. "It's something to do."

"You must be a good swimmer, being on the team and all," she said, looking more closely, I imagined, at my arms and chest.

"He quit this year, though," said Marlene.

"You quit?" said Carmella.

"Well, I *was* on almost all season this year, and since grade school, but I'm not anymore, like Marlene says." I didn't want to get into why, and fortunately Carmella didn't seem curious to know.

"But you *are* swimming the lake?"

"I got nearly halfway last time," I said.

"I'd like to *watch* you sometime." Carmella said this like she was saying she wanted to see me get naked.

"I always go out with Colm—to spot him," Marlene put in. "You could come, too, if you want."

"No," said Carmella, "that's all right. I wouldn't want to interfere." Like Marlene and I were engaged or something.

"It's no interference," said Marlene, not picking up on where Carmella was coming from.

"I don't know if I need anyone to go along anymore, any-way," I said to Marlene, looking at her for the first time since she came up.

She gave me a funny look. "But what if you get in trouble?"

"I'm getting pretty far already without any trouble. I think I can handle it," I said.

Marlene frowned, then something seemed to click and she suddenly said, "Gotta go. You guys have fun," and shoved off.

"'Bye," said Carmella.

I couldn't think of anything right to say after this, and Carmella said nothing. I peeked out of the side of my eyes at her and she was lying there with her eyes open, staring at the sky. Then she stood up. "Let's go in," she said. "It's getting a little too chilly out here," and she dove in and swam for shore.

I went in after her, not feeling so good all of a sudden. When we got back on the beach, Carmella buried her head in a movie magazine and I lay on my stomach, playing with the sand.

I only shot a brief glance out on the lake once or twice the rest of the time we were on the beach, but Marlene must've paddled in or something, 'cause I didn't see her out there. The lake looked empty without her.

"Did I tell you I was learning to drive?" I said—a desperate bit, one I'd been saving as a surprise to tell Carmella when I nearly had the license and when I was sure it would all work out.

"You are?" she said, suddenly all alert, her magazine put down. "When do you get your license?"

"I hope in the next month—before the end of August, anyway. I need to take the test and everything."

"That's great!" she said. "August is the best up at Barstow." And she rolled over and gave me a kiss, on the lips—long and sweet and wet.

That weekend, my father was in some kind of mood. His one-man-all-American-good-guy show looked like it was coming to the end of its run. Maybe it was because he and Mom weren't talking; maybe he had a putrid week, I don't know. But his patience was as thin as the hair on top of his head, which he kept running his hands over during the whole driving lesson, plastering it to his skull.

And so when I hit a pothole hard, he shouted, "Didn't you see that?"

"Yeah," I said, "I tried to go over it. I thought if I went fast enough . . ."

"What do you think this is?" he said. "A movie? This thing doesn't *fly*, damn it!" he said. "I hope you didn't break something." And he made me pull over so he could make a show of huffing around and looking under the car as if he could tell about anything beyond a flat, which fortunately we didn't have.

And if that wasn't good enough, he picked that weekend to try to teach me parallel parking. We used some old, rusted fifty-gallon barrels that were in a parking lot near the lake. A bait shop was there when I was a kid and I remember Dad getting mad at me because I didn't want to touch the nasty-looking sandworms he bought to take us fishing. The place was gone now, burned and bulldozed over, but the lot was still there. Dad got out and rolled a couple of the barrels so they were about a car and a half length apart, and I was supposed to get the car parked between them.

"Dad," I said. "I really don't know if I'm ready for this."

He forced out another tiny dab of cheeriness, like that last sick gob of toothpaste you can get after you take the tube out of the trash basket and squeeze it till it bleeds?

"Don't underestimate yourself, now, Colm. Let's give it a try, anyway, son," he said.

Then he gave me a five-minute (I timed it on the dash-board clock) detailed explanation of how to go about it, from the beginning precise "entry angle" (in degrees) to the final "front and rear check," complete with all the shiftings and clutchings and brakings and wheel turnings so it sounded like I was docking a space shuttle.

This time, I didn't even pretend like I got it.

I pulled up next to the front barrel.

"Too close! Too close!" he barked. "Watch you don't scrape the car. What did I tell you? Leave some air space."

So next time I pulled up too wide.

Then I got it right, but blew it by cutting in too sharp.

Then I got in, but hit the rear barrel, and it took me five

maneuvers and sweating and turning and clutching to get it straightened out.

"Again," said my dad.

And I tried it again, this time coming in too shallow.

"Again." You could see his ears going way red now.

It was like the car and barrels were those little magnetic dogs? First the barrels pulled me in and I couldn't get far enough away, and then I couldn't get close enough. None of this was helped, of course, by having to be all the while furiously pushing down pedals and shifting and turning the wheel and looking over my shoulder. I felt like one of those guys you see on TV, juggling a bowling ball and a machete and a blowtorch. Finally, I gave it too much gas once, missed the barrels entirely, and backed it through one of the rotted logs that were supposed to stop you from driving into the lake.

"The other way! Put it in first; we're sliding down!" But it wouldn't go into first, and I raced the engine in neutral. "Stop! Stop!" Dad yelled as the car started to slide down the bank and he jerked up on the emergency brake between us, exactly as I managed to get it into first, so that the car lurched forward and stalled.

We sat there quiet for a few minutes, the car pointed up so you could see underneath the branches of the trees, my dad with his hand over his face.

"Put it in first," he said after a while. So I did.

"Push down on the clutch pedal." I did this.

"Turn on the ignition." The engine roared to life—over-accelerated.

"Easy," he said. "Let up on the clutch." I felt the car strain against the brake. He released it and we crept forward. Luckily the ground was firm and I was able to get the car up in the lot.

"Let's go," my father said. "That's enough for one day."

We rode in silence for a while. Except, you know how your stomach makes noises after you've eaten a big meal? Well, I could almost hear his brain gurgling with all he wanted to say.

"I don't know if this is going to work," he finally said in a low, matter-of-fact voice. "You simply don't listen. You don't do anything the way I tell you."

"Dad," I said, "it's one thing to tell someone something and another to actually *do* it."

"Don't get wise on me," he said. Wisdom being one of the cardinal sins in the catechism of coaching.

"Dad," I said, frustrated, "that's the first time ever that I even *tried* to park. Give me a little room to make a few mistakes, will you?" and right when I said this, a kid shot out of a drive ahead of us on a skateboard; not looking—probably like I did a hundred times when I was his age—the only thing different being he was about to be a bug on our windshield.

Q: What's the last thing that goes through a skateboarder's mind when he hits your windshield?

A: His skateboard.

"The brake!" my father shouted, but I must've hit the

clutch pedal instead, since I had that sort of weightless feeling you get when you tense up for the Gs but nothing happens. My dad lunged over and hit the horn and the kid tipped up on the sidewalk, and flipped his skateboard and middle finger before taking off.

"That does it," my dad said. "I give up. Get out of there. Let me drive."

I stopped the car and got out. I saw he was going around front and I went that way too. I swear I was going to give him a shove. But we passed each other without bloodshed, got back in the car, and drove off.

The obedient son, once again takes his licks.

Rule 7: "Mistakes" is the name we give to our experiences.

RICH WALLACE, the author of *Wrestling Sturbridge,* grew up in a small New Jersey town where sports were a way of life. He began writing in high school when he kept journals on the highs and lows of his life. Since then he's worked as a sportswriter, news editor, and currently as the coordinating editor of *Highlights* magazine. As the father of two sons, he coaches a variety of youth sports, including soccer. Mr. Wallace now lives in Honesdale, Pennsylvania.

PRAISE FOR *SHOTS ON GOAL*:

"Engrossing fare."

—Kirkus Reviews

"Wallace's ear for locker-room banter and knowledge of fragile adolescent egos shine through in his vibrant characterizations of young contenders."

—Publishers Weekly

"Wallace's characterizations are strong, the teenage 'ambience,' ambivalence, and angst on target. An excellent choice for all those boys who want only sports books, this is also a good read for any teen, male or female, soccer buff or not."

—Booklist

from

SHOTS ON GOAL

BY RICH WALLACE

You sweep it away with the outside of your foot, dodging quickly left, then right, and spurting past the defender. You're as tough as anybody out there, you keep telling yourself, racing now to keep up with the ball.

You need to arc toward the goal, but they're closing in from every angle. You pivot and stumble and the ball bounds away. Now it's whizzing past, waist-high in the opposite direction, and you turn and curse and scramble down the field.

It's mid-September, and the sweat evaporates quickly in the less-humid air. It's easy to breathe hard. You're fifteen, and she's watching, and the blood is close to the surface as you dodge and twist and chase the ball over thick, evenly mowed grass that shines in the slanted light.

Here it comes, shoulder-high but dropping, and you stop it with your chest, bumping it forward and catching it after the first bounce with your foot. Then you've crossed midfield, with running room ahead, and you and the ball and your teammates and the breeze are funneling toward the goal, angling away from the sideline with your chin upraised and eyes open wide.

A stutter-step and an acceleration get you past a defender, and in two more strides you send a long, floating pass toward Joey by the goal. There's contact, a flurry of wrists and knees, and the ball suddenly bullets into the net, beyond the outstretched arms of the goalkeeper.

You drive your fists in exhilaration. Your whole body is a fist, flexed but not tense, and you're as tough as anybody out there. You run and leap and drive your fists again.

You're fifteen and she's watching and you're winning. You're aware of the grass shining in the late afternoon sunlight, of the strength and fatigue in your muscles, and the dryness in your throat you deserve to quench.

Aware of your teammates, of the shouts of the sparsely gathered crowd, and the something in the air that says autumn.

Joey asks me about her after the game, grabbing me lightly above the elbow. "She here to watch you?"

"I don't know." I shrug, pausing, halfway to the locker room. Shannon's standing back by the bleachers with two other girls. She glances my way. My mouth is hanging open.

"You going to the game tonight?" Joey asks, meaning the football game, on the big field downtown.

"Yeah. Why not?" I look around again. She's getting into a car. Joey's started walking again, so I bite on my lip and jog a couple steps to catch him. "You come by for me?"

"I might." Joey's shorter than I am, just as fast, and really is as tough as anybody. He nods. "I'll swing by about seven."

She'll be at the game. Everybody will. I stare at her in the afternoons from the back of the study hall, while she twirls her tawny hair around a finger and reads novels with shiny paper covers. I've seen her watching me, too, as I head for the practice field after school or sit on the hood of a car in the lot.

And I've said hello once or twice, even went as far as "How's it going?" the other day.

She looks at me, too. And she came to the game.

I sit on the bench in front of my locker, pulling off my spikes and examining a long new scratch on my knee. There's a cloud of steam rising from the showers and I strip off my jersey, running my fingers through my damp tangled hair.

Guys are snapping towels and laughing, proud; nobody figured on three straight wins. I grab my towel and a tube of shampoo, pushing the green cage locker shut. Joey's got the tape player on and the floor's wet and I can taste dried sweat on my lips.

The water beats down on my chest and the few wiry hairs there look darker, pressed against my skin. The heat loosens my muscles; there's a whole weekend ahead.

I step into work boots and dungarees and a denim shirt. Joey pokes me in the shoulder and says, "That was a really nice pass, Bones. Catch you later."

I've been coming to Friday night football games at this stadium since I was about seven, sitting high in the bleachers with my father. Tonight I can feel the electricity like never before as me and Joey approach from a side street a few blocks away. The school band is assembled; we hear the thin, brassy music in the distance.

"You watch Bugs Bunny tonight?" Joey asks.

"No. My mother doesn't let us have the TV on when we eat."

He stops walking. "How come in almost every one there's this scene where Elmer Fudd or somebody is chasing Bugs, and Bugs runs into a bedroom to hide, and when Elmer busts in, Bugs is standing there in lacy women's underwear? And then

Bugs screams and Elmer slams the door and blushes."

"Sounds familiar." I kind of pull him on the shoulder and we start walking again.

"They had one of the really old ones on," he says. "Porky Pig, of all people, is out hunting and he thinks Bugs gets shot. So Porky tries to do CPR, but he has to pry Bugs's hands off his chest, and when he does, you see that Bugs has a bra on. So Bugs screams and jumps up, and he flutters away like a ballerina or something." Joey puts his hands up and wriggles his fingers and takes some little prancy sidesteps.

"You do that good," I say.

He frowns. "I was demonstrating."

"So, what are you saying? He's . . . what?"

"I think he likes it. I think maybe he bats left-handed now and then."

I shrug. "He's an actor."

"Yeah, but you can tell he's enjoying it. I think he's a transvestite."

I put my hands over my ears and fake like I'm horror-stricken.

We've reached the field. It's bright and noisy, as if all the town's energy is compressed into this bowl. The stands are just about full.

We sit near midfield, ten rows up. I'm wearing a blue windbreaker with the school's name and a soccer ball decaled on the back. The teams are warming up on the field.

It looks like Joey shaved. He's got his glasses on tonight, so he looks kind of refined. He's wearing the same jacket I am.

Shannon's down there by the fence, alone, looking up at the crowd. I catch her eye and lift a finger in recognition, and there's no question that her face brightens. Any room? she mouths, and I nod with my whole face and wave her up.

Joey shifts to the left, I shift to the right, and she's sitting where I want her, soft and firm on the concrete bleachers. She's the best contribution to the mix of cigar smoke and powder and cologne under lights that are brighter than daylight.

I try not to smile too wide as she squeezes in, but I'm almost laughing with happiness. She says something to Joey about a history assignment, and he smirks and waves it off. "I'll do it the night before it's due," he says.

She's got on this tan kind of coat and a dark shirt underneath, and she seems somehow livelier than I've ever seen in school. She waves to two of her friends who are walking down below, and they make faces at her like *We can see what you're up to, honey.*

"You played really well today," she says, poking me on the arm.

"Not bad," I say, pumping up a little more.

⚽   ⚽   ⚽

Fourth quarter comes and we've been laughing for most of the game, me and her. But the Pepsi I bought at halftime needs to escape, so I get up and head for the bathroom, pushing through the crowd.

I bump into Herbie the goalie with some others from the team. "Hanging out later?" he asks.

"Yeah, I'd say so." I've got on a wry kind of smile, hands in the pockets of my windbreaker.

"We're hitting McDonald's after the game. You up for it?"

"Think I'll pass. I got other plans."

"Yeah, I saw you up there with her. Decent."

"Well, I gotta go," I say. "I'll talk to you tomorrow."

I get back to the stands and offer her some M&Ms. She takes two red ones. Our school is ahead by a couple of touchdowns. When the game ends I kind of nudge her. "You wanna, you know, go get something to eat or something?"

She looks a little embarrassed all of a sudden. "Oh. Didn't Joey tell you?"

"Tell me what?"

"Well, I asked him to take me out after the game." She smiles, tilting her head just a bit in consolation. "Sorry."

I look at Joey and my mouth hangs open again. Joey looks down at his shoes, then out at the field.

"Oh," Shannon says in a hurry, "why don't you come along?"

I bite down on my lip, scanning the crowd. "Nah . . . I see Herbie over there. I'll catch up to him and see what's going on. Thanks anyway. See ya."

Sure I will.

I walk down the bleachers and head to where Herbie and the other guys are, glancing back once to see her and Joey walking up toward street level. I stand around while Herbie and the others bust chops, staring out across the field to the highway, at the traffic headed for home.

I inch away from the group, toward the exit at the far end of the stadium. The band is still playing the fight song, but it's far away now. I'm numb.

I shuffle through the excited crowd, out the gate in a hurry. After two blocks I'm clear of the lights and the sounds of the stadium, my boots kicking up the first fallen leaves of the season. I begin to run easy, to get the feeling back, and bite down on my lip.

Joey hadn't said ten words the whole game. I'd been at my best; I had things to say, for once. Her warm brown eyes held some genuine interest. She'd been at the game this afternoon.

I move into the street to pass a guy walking home from the stadium with his little boy, no more than seven.

I pass by the school, dark and closed, and now I'm running faster, hopping the curb to cross a side street. The sweat is starting under my clothes, and I shake my hair back out of my eyes. I dodge quickly left, then right, chin upraised and defiant. A stutter-step and an acceleration get me past the defender, urging the ball ahead, my eyes taking in the whole field but focused on that area of ground between me and the sideline.

There's running room ahead, but they're closing in from every angle. You're tough, as tough as anybody out there, taking in the grunts of the opponents, struggling with unskilled feet to work the ball down the field; so keenly aware of the immediate space you need to conquer, less sharply aware of the goal.

⚽   ⚽   ⚽

My bedroom is in the back corner of the upstairs, across the hall from my brother Tommy's. I'm lying on my bed, staring at the ceiling, thinking about our next game. It's hard to believe that we're 3–0. We went 2–11–1 a year ago. Suddenly we're 3–0.

Nobody can believe it. Not to say that many people have noticed, of course. Not in this town.

We've got our fourth one on Tuesday, a home game against the defending league champions. Last year they shut us out both times, 7–0 and 5–0, when we had five freshmen starting and they had mostly seniors. Now we're sophomores and we're undefeated. But we'll be lucky if forty people show up to watch the game. I've seen forty people at one time in the bathroom at a wrestling match. Sturbridge is a football and wrestling town.

My brother wrestles. Tommy's been varsity since his freshman year; placed second in the state last winter, and he's still only a junior. But he and I are different. Lots different.

Tommy lives in the here and now. He's direct. He makes sense when he talks. I narrate my life as it occurs. I have conversations in my head, and I forget sometimes what I've said aloud and what I've only practiced saying in my mind. I get myself in trouble that way, with girls, with teachers, with my friends.

My mother sticks her head in the doorway and smiles at me. "Whatcha thinking about, Barry?" she asks.

"Nothing," I say. "Soccer."

She walks into the room and looks at the pictures on the wall by the window. I've got photographs from every team I've ever been on—two years of Little League, three seasons of Biddy Basketball, about ten seasons of indoor and outdoor soccer at the Y.

"Ever talk much with Carrie?" Mom asks, pointing to a girl kneeling next to me in one of the soccer photos.

I shake my head. "No."

"Seems like a nice girl." This is a nudge, but I won't bite.

"I guess," I say. "She's going out with a senior."

"Oh." She turns toward me and smiles again, brushing back her hair, which is dark and sort of curly. She's worried about me. I'm too into sports, I only have one close friend, I spend a lot of time in my room with the door shut, and I've never had a girl-friend. That's what she sees, anyway.

"Come downstairs soon," she says. "Don't waste a Sunday afternoon."

She leaves and I get up and close the door. I sit on the bed and look at the wall.

Joey's in just about every picture; his father coached every-thing and I almost always landed on his team because me and Joey have been best friends since second grade. But it was never Joey's team, or my team, or the Sharks or the Jets or the Blasters—whatever the official name was that season—it was Bones-and-Joey's team. Always. An inseparable partnership.

Joey was the star of those teams, scoring lots of goals, mak-ing the lay-up off the fast break, driving in the winning run. I was the guy who made Joey look good, taking the outlet pass and finding him in the clear, or crossing the ball in front of the goal so he could knock it in.

I'm still doing it. He's got five goals this season and I've assisted on four of them. It also looks like he's got a girlfriend, and I think I deserve a double assist for that one. The jerk.

My life has been lived within two shadows: my brother's and Joey's. Even my name, what everybody calls me and doesn't really fit, came from Tommy. His first sentence, the legend goes, was "Boney wet," Boney being his fifteen-month-old pronunciation of Barry. It stuck, although I've never been particularly boney. I'm five-foot-seven, 140.

Joey's shadow is different. He and I have always been there for each other. Until the other night, I mean. First fight I ever got in was during second-grade recess. We were playing touch football and I was mostly blocking. This kid Steven Bittner—who was twice my size—kept trying to to get past me. Finally I got mad enough and swung at him, and he whacked me good in the teeth. Then he pinned me down and had his knees on my shoulders, and Joey yelled, "Let him up, you pig!"

Steven turned his head to look at Joey, and I started squirming like crazy to get out from underneath.

"Let him up," Joey said. "He can't fight like that."

So Steven started to get off me. He was big and slow, and I was small and fast. I got to my knees real quick and caught him square in the nose with my fist. By then some teachers had noticed the commotion and started running over. Steven and I had to stay in for the next week of recesses, but he never bothered me again.

Joey's always been a half-step ahead of me in sports, but we've been on even ground in everything else.

He just took a step past me with Shannon, though. And I don't think that's fair.

JENNIFER ARMSTRONG is the author of several highly praised books for children, including the picture books *Chin Yu Min and the Ginger Cat* and *Hugh Can Do* and the novels *Steal Away*, *Black-Eyed Susan*, and *The Dreams of Mairhe Mehan*, the prequel to *Mary Mehan Awake*.

She lives with her husband in Saratoga Springs, New York.

PRAISE FOR *MARY MEHAN AWAKE*:

"The story unfolds effortlessly and richly. . . . It's *The Secret Garden* for an older audience."

—The Horn Book

PRAISE FOR *THE DREAMS OF MAIRHE MEHAN*:

★ "A finely wrought historical novel...remarkable for its artistry and the lingering musicality of its language."

—Publishers Weekly (starred review)

♦ "A haunting, eloquent story...Armstrong mixes vision and reality with breat-taking virtuosity, salting Mairhe's narrative with poetic turns of phrase, snatches of song, story, and history."

—Kirkus Reviews (pointer review)

"This is a work to be savored...a powerfully poetic tale."

—School Library Journal

A *Bulletin of the Center for Children's Books* Blue Ribbon Book
A *Hungry Mind Review* Children's Book of Distinction

from MARY MEHAN AWAKE

BY JENNIFER ARMSTRONG

THUNDER

GRACE HARBOR WAS visited by a thunderstorm on a night late in May. Behind the large white house, where Dorsett had established a blind from which to photograph nesting bluebirds, the maples turned their leaves against the wind. The vine-covered gazebo shuddered under the pelting rain. In the vegetable garden, water ran between the furrows, seeking pea seeds that strained up through the mud. On the lake, the heaving water sprayed upward toward the clouds. The two small boats in the boat house bumped and knocked against their moorings. Racing sheets of rain swept down the windows of the house.

At the top of the stairs, lightning flashed through the oval window and brought the stuffed birds and mounted butterflies to momentary life, and sent sparks through the case filled with crystals. Gleams of lightning struck rainbows from the prisms of

MARY MEHAN AWAKE

the dining room chandelier. Light darted over the stags' antlers and sent shadows like tree branches leaping across the downstairs hall.

The thunder knocked on the doors, making the finches hop nervously in their cage. It rattled the windows in their frames, as though trying to rouse the house from a deep sleep. Then it rolled over the rooftop and down the chimneys, waking Mary.

She lay in her bed in the dark, and in the flashes of lightning saw the shape of the books stacked beside her bed; they were books Henry had lent to her. Each thump and mutter of thunder told her that Henry was sleeping in his room above the carriage house, unaware of the storm, and she said out loud into the darkness, I must tell him about the thunder tomorrow, he will want to know.

A curious pattern had developed. When no one else was nearby, Mary spoke to Henry of her past life in Washington, where she had worked as a barmaid and a nurse; she spoke to him about her brother killed in the war and the father she had worked to send back to Ireland. These things she had to say out loud, but she did not want anyone to hear. She hoarded her voice like a miser with everyone else; with Henry, she spent it recklessly.

The things she heard, she told Henry of in notes and letters. In the kitchen, eating supper with Rose wheezing at the head of the table, Mary would write to him, *Mr. Dorsett was practicing bird calls in the darkroom today. He is very proud of his wood duck call.*

Mrs. Dorsett has hung in her window a string of shells from her cousins in Jamaica—they clink and tinkle when the breeze comes off the lake.

I think there are mice in the east wall of my room: there is a scratching sometimes in the night.

Rose has sniffles again. When she blows her nose, it honks.

Eating, Henry would watch her write, listening to the sounds she wrote. Sometimes he would write briefly, *Bacon frying is a good sound,* or *I think that red hen must be a noisy complainer—is she?*

Mary began to collect sounds for Henry. She gave him as many as she could.

In return, he let her talk and did not ask what she was saying. He gave her books. He showed her where the vegetable plants were sprouting in the garden, and once took her to see a nest of baby mice he had discovered in the barn. Sometimes, in an offhand way, he handed her a flower if he had been gardening, or a spray of mint, or a small crystal unearthed among the pea vines.

What do you hear? he would write to her when they crossed paths during the day.

And Mary would stop, and listen, and write, *Pot lids in the kitchen,* or *Mrs. Dorsett singing as she walks up the staircase,* or *Waves from the beach,* or *The coffee grinder has as many noises as beans; Rose is cranking it hard.*

So even as Mary lay awake listening to the thunder, she was telling Henry about the sound, the knock and tumble of it, the growl and mutter, and about how it had awoken her from a dreamless sleep.

Henry will want to know, she told her darkened room.

But as it happened, she had more than that to tell him in the morning. Dorsett called her into his study before breakfast, and there told her the errand he wanted her—and Henry—to do. They were to take Dorsett's collection of stuffed warblers to the Niagara Falls Seminary for Women, a small school run by a colleague of his. The birds were to be on loan for the day to illustrate the principles of differentiation among species, and although Dorsett had planned to take them himself, he had changed his mind: he wanted to spend the day in his blind, trying to photograph the bluebirds. Therefore, Mary and Henry were to go, and while the school was using the warblers, they would be free to visit the falls. They were well worth visiting, Dorsett assured Mary with a smile, and only twenty miles away from Grace Harbor.

And so it was that by noon, having taken the spur line to

the city of Niagara Falls and delivered the warblers in their cases to the seminary, Mary and Henry walked over a stone footbridge to Goat Island. Beneath the bridge, the turbulent flood of the Niagara River pouring out of Lake Erie foamed and bubbled around rocks, and whole tree trunks, dark and saturated with water, slammed against the banks before rushing on. Gulls wheeled screaming overhead.

Mary paused to watch the hypnotic rush of water. In the distance was another sound that she tipped her head to hear, an indistinct roar that seemed to come from all directions at once, almost as though it were the sound of the sunshine that flooded the area. Henry leaned on his elbows on the wall of the bridge.

Have you seen this waterfall before? Mary wrote. *Is it very big?*

Henry grinned as he read her question. *Haven't you ever heard of Niagara Falls?* Mary shook her head. *You'll see for yourself, then. What do you hear?*

I don't know. I don't know what it is.

He nodded his head toward the tree-covered island, and they walked on. Other tourists strolled by them, talking eagerly together, and vendors called out to hawk panoramic postcards, souvenir spoons, beaded Indian moccasins, peanuts and candy. Gulls were everywhere, arguing over bread scraps and heckling the tourists. And over all was the one great sound, growing louder and louder with each step Mary took along the path.

A feeling of apprehension began to take hold of her. She stopped where the path began to curve around a screen of trees. The noise was all around them.

Henry walked on ahead, not realizing she had stopped.

Mary's heart began to race. "What is that?" she whispered. "What is that noise?"

She moved forward slowly. As she rounded the corner, she saw Henry stopped in his tracks, and beyond him was the roaring cataract. Mary reeled backward slightly as she took it in, the impossible, giant cascade of water falling into the gorge far below. The cloud of mist rising from the torrent was like the steam from some titanic machine, and the flying gulls disappeared into it, tiny specks swallowed by the vapor.

"I didn't know," Mary stammered. She shielded her eyes against the sun with one hand, and with the other groped blindly for something to hold on to. She touched a railing and stood there, shaking her head.

A man climbing up the path gave her a look of concern. "Taken queer, are you? It takes many folks that way. Just catch your breath and you'll be on the gain in no time."

Mary kept shaking her head. "I didn't know it was so...big."

"That's the Canadian side of the falls, the Horseshoe," the man said with a sweep of his arm. "Hundred and sixty feet straight down. What you see there is the Great Lakes falling over a cliff. Say, is that your beau down there?"

Mary saw him pointing at Henry, and shook her head quickly. "Oh, no, no. He is my friend."

"Well, he looks like he might be taken a little queer, too; I'd watch out for him. Never even looked at me when I told him to mind the steps."

Mary didn't bother to explain, but hurried down the path to join Henry where he stood at the railing. He looked down at her with a smile, and Mary nodded. Then they turned to regard the falls, their faces bathed in mist.

The river above the precipice boiled and plunged headlong through the rapids, foaming blue-green. The ceaseless, relentless surge of the water was mesmerizing, and where it flowed over the edge into space it seemed almost to stand still. The sound was monstrous, and the wind the falls created buffeted Mary where she stood. She clutched the wet iron railing, staring and staring at the flow. Mist clung to her lashes, and she blinked it away.

Henry passed his notebook to her. *This goes on and on forever, no matter what men do in the world. It does not know mankind or our fights.*

Mary looked at the waterfall, looked at Henry, looked at the waterfall again. *Then I am glad for it being here,* she wrote.

There is a staircase to the bottom of the American Falls. I'd like to show you the cave there. Would you care to go down?

Almost in a daze, Mary nodded. She followed Henry along the edge of the rocky island that split the Niagara River in two and sent it cascading into the Niagara Gorge. The place was crowded with sightseers, and Mary was vaguely aware of a gabble of foreign languages, shrieks of excitement and cries of admiration, but it was all muted and dwarfed by the giant sound of the waterfall thundering into the chasm. Ahead was a painted wooden booth with a sign above, "Biddle Stairs: Cave of the Winds." Farther along was another plume of mist and spray rising from the second cataract, the American Falls. At the side of the booth, people were shrugging into full-length oilskin coats, laughing and joking and teasing one another in anticipation. A white-haired man was selling hot coffee from a pushcart to the wet and breathless tourists who pulled themselves up from down below. Shouts of "Oh, there's the top at last!" and "What a climb!" floated up the stairs with the mist.

"Like to brave the mighty waterfall in the Cave of the Winds, mister? Dollar per person," the man in the booth called out to Henry.

"He can't hear you," Mary said. She touched Henry's arm and pointed at the sign. Henry nodded. "We'll both go down," she added.

"Two dollars. Mind the wet. The stairs are plenty slippery, young lady. Step around to the side and find a coat that fits you," the man said. "Tell your friend to do the same."

As Mary moved to the side of the little building, she saw the Biddle Stairs, which were more a narrow wooden ladder than a staircase. The rickety structure snaked down the face of the cliff, secured with rusting iron bolts. Twenty yards away, the American Falls poured down the same cliff with a deafening roar. Mary peeked over the edge. Gusts of wind surged up into her face, but below she could see a narrow, glistening path hugging the rock, leading toward the cataract. She felt a touch on her shoulder, and turned to see Henry holding out a coat for her. She put it on, its damp weight pressing on her shoulders. Her fingers trembled as she fastened the buttons.

Now that Henry's notebook was stowed in a dry pocket, communication was impossible. They exchanged a look, and then began to descend. Each tread of the steep staircase was slick with water, and the railing dripped at the touch. Mary used one hand to keep her skirts out of the way as she climbed down. Nodding grasses poked out of the cliff face between the treads, and with each step Mary took, more and more of the American Falls came into view. The sound grew louder and more explosive the lower she went, and she felt the staircase shake with the force of the winds. Gusts of mist and spray blew against her. Her heart was pounding, but when Henry looked up at her, she found herself smiling in spite of her fear. Water dripped from his eyelashes and sparkled in the sunlight.

At the bottom, Henry reached up to help her down the

last step. Their wet hands met for a moment, and then Mary hugged her oilskin coat tighter before they set off down the wet path. Puddles shone in the sun. Water dripped and trickled from a hundred fissures and cracks in the rock face. Huge boulders and bare broken tree trunks lay in gleaming, jumbled piles, and gulls circled above them, their cries drowned by the stupendous thunder of the falls.

At last, they reached the base of the waterfall, where the treacherous path led behind the cascade. The world was all water, pouring from above. Mary tipped her face up and was immediately drenched by splashes and mist. Then she drew a deep breath and stepped behind the face of the waterfall.

The path snaked around a boulder and suddenly opened into the Cave of the Winds. Mary and Henry stood amazed, bracing themselves against the strong swirling currents of air. The face of the cave was a solid wall of cascading blue-green water, and the western sun shining through it created a thousand circular rainbows that spangled and spun through the echoing cavern. Mary turned around and around, watching the rainbows, feeling herself swallowed by the terrible grandeur of the waterfall. The air was so thick with mist that she could hardly breathe. Never in her life had she imagined anything so overwhelming, so tremendous, as being inside a waterfall; never had she thought that nature could contain so much water, or that she could stand below it as it fell, a magnificent absolution. The very air and rocks vibrated with the power of the water, making the sound something that was inside Mary.

The thunder of the falls filled her, surrounded her, shook her and deafened her, and she knew she could hear no more than Henry could. She was as deaf as he was. She looked at him, dripping, his face shining with exhilaration as he gazed upon the sheet of water, and the giant sound pounded inside her until she found she was shouting as loud as she could.

"Henry! Henry!" she cried out, knowing that he could never hear her, unable to hear herself. "Henry!" And even as she yelled, she knew she wanted, more than anything, for him to hear the sound of her voice saying his name.

PHILIP PULLMAN is the author of the acclaimed *The Golden Compass* and *The Subtle Knife*, the first two volumes in the trilogy *His Dark Materials*. He is also the author of *Count Karlstein* (Knopf, Fall 1998) and a trilogy of Victorian thrillers featuring Sally Lockhart: *The Ruby in the Smoke*, *Shadow in the North*, and *The Tiger in the Well*.

A graduate of Oxford University with a degree in English, Philip Pullman has written novels, plays, and picture books for readers of all ages. He lives with his family in England, where he is hard at work on the final book in the *His Dark Materials* trilogy.

THE GOLDEN COMPASS

PRAISE FOR *THE GOLDEN COMPASS*:

★ "Breathtaking...As always, Pullman is a master at combining impeccable characterizations and seamless plotting, maintaining a crackling pace to create scene upon scene of almost unbearable tension. This glittering gem will leave readers of all ages eagerly awaiting the next installment of Lyra's adventures."

—*Publishers Weekly* (starred review)

♦ "This first fantastic installment propels readers along with horror and high adventure...a shattering tale that begins with a promise and delivers an entire universe."

—*Kirkus Reviews* (pointer review)

"Superb...wonder-filled. Pullman offers moral complexity as well as heart-stopping adventures."

—*The Washington Post*

The Carnegie Medal (England)
An ALA Notable Children's Book
An ALA Top Ten Best Book for Young Adults
A *Publishers Weekly* Best Book of the Year

from
THE GOLDEN COMPASS

BY PHILIP PULLMAN

As they reached the first of the houses, Lyra looked to the right and left, peering hard into the dimness, for the Aurora was fading and the moon still far from rising. Here and there a light flickered under a snow-thick roof, and Lyra thought she saw pale faces behind some of the windowpanes, and imagined their astonishment to see a child riding a great white bear.

At the center of the little village there was an open space next to the jetty, where boats had been drawn up, mounds under the snow. The noise of the dogs was deafening, and just as Lyra thought it must have wakened everyone, a door opened and a man came out holding a rifle. His wolverine dæmon leaped onto the woodstack beside the door, scattering snow.

Lyra slipped down at once and stood between him and Iorek Byrnison, conscious that she had told the bear there was no need for his armor.

The man spoke in words she couldn't understand. Iorek Byrnison replied in the same language, and the man gave a little moan of fear.

"He thinks we are devils," Iorek told Lyra. "What shall I say?"

"Tell him we're not devils, but we've got friends who are. And we're looking for . . . Just a child. A strange child. Tell him that."

As soon as the bear had said that, the man pointed to the right, indicating some place further off, and spoke quickly.

Iorek Byrnison said, "He asks if we have come to take the child away. They are afraid of it. They have tried to drive it away, but it keeps coming back."

"Tell him we'll take it away with us, but they were very bad to treat it like that. Where is it?"

The man explained, gesticulating fearfully. Lyra was afraid he'd fire his rifle by mistake, but as soon as he'd spoken he hastened inside his house and shut the door. Lyra could see faces at every window.

"Where is the child?" she said.

"In the fish house," the bear told her, and turned to pad down toward the jetty.

Lyra followed. She was horribly nervous. The bear was making for a narrow wooden shed, raising his head to sniff this way and that, and when he reached the door he stopped and said: "In there."

Lyra's heart was beating so fast she could hardly breathe. She raised her hand to knock at the door and then, feeling that that was ridiculous, took a deep breath to call out, but realized that she didn't know what to say. Oh, it was so dark now! She should have brought a lantern. . . .

There was no choice, and anyway, she didn't want the bear to see her being afraid. He had spoken of mastering his fear: that was what she'd have to do. She lifted the strap of reindeer hide holding the latch in place, and tugged hard against the frost binding the door shut. It opened with a snap. She had to kick aside the snow piled against the foot of the door before she could pull it open, and Pantalaimon was no help, running back and forth in his ermine shape, a white shadow over the white ground, uttering little frightened sounds.

"Pan, for God's sake!" she said. "Be a bat. Go and *look* for me.... "

But he wouldn't, and he wouldn't speak either. She had never seen him like this except once, when she and Roger in the crypt at Jordan had moved the dæmon-coins into the wrong skulls. He was even more frightened than she was. As for Iorek Byrnison, he was lying in the snow nearby, watching in silence.

"Come out," Lyra said as loud as she dared. "Come out!"

Not a sound came in answer. She pulled the door a little wider, and Pantalaimon leaped up into her arms, pushing and pushing at her in his cat form, and said, "Go away! Don't stay here! Oh, Lyra, go now! Turn back!"

Trying to hold him still, she was aware of Iorek Byrnison getting to his feet, and turned to see a figure hastening down the track from the village, carrying a lantern. When he came close enough to speak, he raised the lantern and held it to show his face: an old man with a broad, lined face, and eyes nearly lost in a thousand wrinkles. His dæmon was an arctic fox.

He spoke, and Iorek Byrnison said:

"He says that it's not the only child of that kind. He's seen others in the forest. Sometimes they die quickly, sometimes they don't die. This one is tough, he thinks. But it would be better for him if he died."

"Ask him if I can borrow his lantern," Lyra said.

The bear spoke, and the man handed it to her at once, nodding vigorously. She realized that he'd come down in order to bring it to her, and thanked him, and he nodded again and stood back, away from her and the hut and away from the bear.

Lyra thought suddenly: What if the child is Roger? And she prayed with all her force that it wouldn't be. Pantalaimon was clinging to her, an ermine again, his little claws hooked deep into her anorak.

She lifted the lantern high and took a step into the shed, and then she saw what it was that the Oblation Board was doing, and what was the nature of the sacrifice the children were having to make.

The little boy was huddled against the wood drying rack where hung row upon row of gutted fish, all as stiff as boards. He was clutching a piece of fish to him as Lyra was clutching Pantalaimon, with her left hand, hard, against her heart; but that was all he had, a piece of dried fish; because he had no dæmon at all. The Gobblers had cut it away. That was *intercision*, and this was a severed child.

Her first impulse was to turn and run, or to be sick. A human being with no dæmon was like someone without a face, or with their ribs laid open and their heart torn out: something unnatural and uncanny that belonged to the world of night-ghasts, not the waking world of sense.

So Lyra clung to Pantalaimon and her head swam and her gorge rose, and cold as the night was, a sickly sweat moistened her flesh with something colder still.

"Ratter," said the boy. "You got my Ratter?"

Lyra was in no doubt what he meant.

"No," she said in a voice as frail and frightened as she felt. Then, "What's your name?"

"Tony Makarios," he said. "Where's Ratter?"

"I don't know . . ." she began, and swallowed hard to govern her nausea. "The Gobblers..." But she couldn't finish. She had to go out of the shed and sit down by herself in the snow, except that of course she wasn't by herself, she was never by herself, because Pantalaimon was always there. Oh, to be cut from him as this little boy had been parted from his Ratter! The worst thing in the world! She found herself sobbing, and Pantalaimon was whimpering too, and in both of them there was a passionate pity and sorrow for the half-boy.

Then she got to her feet again.

"Come on," she called in a trembling voice. "Tony, come out. We're going to take you somewhere safe."

There was a stir of movement in the fish house, and he appeared at the door, still clutching his dried fish. He was dressed in warm enough garments, a thickly padded and quilted coal-silk anorak and fur boots, but they had a secondhand look and didn't fit well. In the wider light outside that came from the faint trails of the Aurora and the snow-covered ground he looked more lost and piteous even than he had at first, crouching in the lantern light by the fish racks.

The villager who'd brought the lantern had retreated a few yards, and called down to them.

Iorek Byrnison interpreted: "He says you must pay for that fish."

Lyra felt like telling the bear to kill him, but she said, "We're taking the child away for them. They can afford to give one fish to pay for that."

The bear spoke. The man muttered, but didn't argue. Lyra set his lantern down in the snow and took the half-boy's hand to guide him to the bear. He came helplessly, showing no surprise and no fear at the great white beast standing so close, and when Lyra helped him to sit on Iorek's back, all he said was:

"I dunno where my Ratter is."

"No, nor do we, Tony," she said. "But we'll...We'll punish the Gobblers. We'll do that, I promise. Iorek, is it all right if I sit up there too?"

"My armor weighs far more than children," he said.

So she scrambled up behind Tony and made him cling to the long, stiff fur, and Pantalaimon sat inside her hood, warm and close and full of pity. Lyra knew that Pantalaimon's impulse was to reach out and cuddle the little half-child, to lick him and gentle him and warm him as his own dæmon would have done; but the great taboo prevented that, of course.

They rose through the village and up toward the ridge, and the villagers' faces were open with horror and a kind of fearful relief at seeing that hideously mutilated creature taken away by a girl and a great white bear.

In Lyra's heart, revulsion struggled with compassion, and compassion won. She put her arms around the skinny little form to hold him safe. The journey back to the main party was colder, and harder, and darker, but it seemed to pass more quickly for all that. Iorek Byrnison was tireless, and Lyra's riding became automatic, so that she was never in danger of falling off. The cold body in her arms was so light that in one way he was easy to manage, but he was inert; he sat stiffly without moving as the bear moved, so in another way he was difficult too.

From time to time the half-boy spoke.

"What's that you said?" asked Lyra.

"I says is she gonna know where I am?"

"Yeah, she'll know, she'll find you and we'll find her. Hold on tight now, Tony. It en't far from here...."

The bear loped onward. Lyra had no idea how tired she was until they caught up with the gyptians. The sledges had stopped to rest the dogs, and suddenly there they all were, Farder Coram,

Lord Faa, Lee Scoresby, all lunging forward to help and then falling back silent as they saw the other figure with Lyra. She was so stiff that she couldn't even loosen her arms around his body, and John Faa himself had to pull them gently open and lift her off.

"Gracious God, what is this?" he said. "Lyra, child, what have you found?"

"He's called Tony," she mumbled through frozen lips. "And they cut his dæmon away. That's what the Gobblers do."

The men held back, fearful; but the bear spoke, to Lyra's weary amazement, chiding them.

"Shame on you! Think what this child has done! You might not have more courage, but you should be ashamed to show less."

"You're right, Iorek Byrnison," said John Faa, and turned to give orders. "Build that fire up and heat some soup for the child. For both children. Farder Coram, is your shelter rigged?"

"It is, John. Bring her over and we'll get her warm...."

"And the little boy," said someone else. "He can eat and get warm, even if..."

Lyra was trying to tell John Faa about the witches, but they were all so busy, and she was so tired. After a confusing few minutes full of lantern light, woodsmoke, and figures hurrying to and fro, she felt a gentle nip on her ear from Pantalaimon's ermine teeth, and woke to find the bear's face a few inches from hers.

"The witches," Pantalaimon whispered. "I called Iorek."

"Oh, yeah," she mumbled. "Iorek, thank you for taking me there and back. I might not remember to tell Lord Faa about the witches, so you better do that instead of me."

She heard the bear agree, and then she fell asleep properly.

SUSAN SHREVE is the author of more than twenty popular books for children, including *The Flunking of Joshua T. Bates*; *Joshua T. Bates Takes Charge*; *Lucy Forever & Miss Rosetree, Shrinks*; and *The Goalie*.

Ms. Shreve has four children and lives with her husband in Washington, D.C., where she is a professor of English at George Mason University.

PRAISE FOR *THE FLUNKING OF JOSHUA T. BATES*:

"Touching, funny, and realistic."

—*School Library Journal*

"Crisply humorous."

—*The Bulletin of the Center for Children's Books*

PRAISE FOR *JOSHUA T. BATES TAKES CHARGE*:

"A perceptive story that makes it plain what it's like to be an outcast and also what it takes to be a hero. Welcome back, Joshua!"

—*Booklist*

from

Joshua T. Bates
In Trouble Again

by SUSAN SHREVE

Joshua's first day in fourth grade was not going well.

First there was the problem with the goons and then the cigarette and then he flunked a math quiz first period and everyone in the class knew about it.

To Joshua's horror, the quizzes were corrected in class. Everyone traded papers with the person sitting on his or her right and Mr. Regan read the answers. Rusty traded papers with Joshua. Rusty got a 90 and Joshua got a 30.

"Never mind, Joshua," Mr. Regan said after the scores had been read out. "This material is new to you."

But he did mind, of course. It didn't matter whether the material was new to him or not, now everyone in the class knew he got a 30 on a math quiz, which was not a good way to begin fourth grade when he already had a reputation for flunking third.

At least when the bell rang for the next period, Tommy Wilhelm leaned over in a friendly sort of way and told Joshua to meet him by the lower field at recess and they'd play soccer if it wasn't raining. And Rusty went with him to social studies so Joshua didn't have to walk down the corridor alone.

"Do you think Regan will tell the principal about the cigarette?" Rusty asked just loud enough to be heard by the fourth-grade girls walking ahead of them. They looked back at Joshua and giggled.

"Tell the principal?" Joshua asked, alarmed. "I never thought of that. Why would he?"

"Dunno," Rusty said. "You never know about Regan. He can be a grizzly."

"I hope he doesn't," Joshua said, following Rusty into the library, where social studies was held. "That would ruin my life."

Rusty shrugged. "Probably not ruin it completely."

In social studies Joshua couldn't concentrate on Russia. He didn't feel right. Not sick necessarily, but as if he might soon be sick. He was uncomfortable, aware of the way he looked in his father's huge shirt, how small his hands were, aware of his classmates watching him. They were probably thinking, "Joshua Bates is still stupid." He was afraid that the teacher, a tall stork of a woman with white feathery hair and a lisp, would recommend that he return to third grade because he couldn't concentrate on Russia.

He wondered if Mrs. Goodwin had heard about the cigarette. He certainly hoped she had not. He owed Mrs. Goodwin everything for helping him get promoted, teaching him to read and write and even spell, which he'd never been able to do. He couldn't bear to disappoint her. Before recess, he decided, he'd have to tell her that the cigarette was an accident, sort of a joke, that he hadn't meant to cause trouble.

And before he realized he had been daydreaming, drawing pictures of cats on his social studies notebook, the stork woman was standing right next to him at the library table.

"You are Joshua Bates. Correct?" she asked.

"Yes," Joshua said.

"I understand from Mrs. Goodwin that you did extremely well in third grade and have been promoted to our class."

Joshua nodded.

"That's very nice and we're pleased to have you," she said in her funny, floating voice. But she didn't sound very pleased at all. She sounded as if she was going to say something unpleasant, something critical, and suddenly Joshua imagined himself saying out loud in front of everybody, "Listen, bean brain. Tell the truth. You're not glad to see me at all."

In fact, he wondered if he *had* said it.

He checked her face for signs of anger.

"One of the rules in my class is to pay attention." She seemed to be screaming, her mouth opened wide in a bird-like yawn, her lips in an O. He was sure that the secretaries in the principal's office across the hall and even the principal could hear her shouting and would know that Joshua T. Bates was in trouble again.

"I don't expect you to know about Russian history since you just arrived, but I expect you to listen," the stork woman said.

"I was listening," Joshua said. "I was listening hard."

"I beg your pardon?" she asked.

"I said I was listening."

He shouldn't have said that, of course. He should have nodded and smiled and said he was sorry to have fallen into a daydream in her class. But he didn't and suddenly the stork woman seemed to expand like an angry bird, growing and growing until she looked to him as if she were filling the entire library with her bad temper.

When the bell rang for recess, Joshua followed Rusty out of the classroom.

"Is that what she's always like?" he asked Rusty.

"Miss Perry?" Rusty shrugged. "She likes girls better than boys," he said. "Tomorrow, come in a dress."

"Right," Joshua said, stopping by Mrs. Goodwin's classroom. "I'll borrow one of Amanda's." He laughed. But he was not really amused. In fact, he felt terrible and wanted to go home. "See you later," he called, watching Rusty fling his arm over Ethan's shoulder and head to the playground.

Joshua needed to talk to Mrs. Goodwin. He desperately needed to talk to her right away, but when he looked through the glass window on the door to the classroom, there was another student standing beside her desk, a girl who seemed to be crying. He caught Mrs. Goodwin's attention and waved.

"Later," she called. "Maybe after school."

And Joshua felt his own eyes fill with tears.

Every school day since the beginning of his second time in third grade, he had been with Mrs. Goodwin, her special project, her best student, her pride and joy. They had worked hours and hours together after school at her house, talked before school and after school and during recess. Anytime he needed her, she was there. Joshua came first before anyone else.

For a moment he watched her talk to the little girl with short brown curls rubbing her eyes. That was the way Mrs. Goodwin was—nothing mushy, no hugging or kissing or "I'm so sorry." She just listened and talked. It broke his heart to see her talking to someone else the way she had always talked to him.

He checked the clock over the library door. Already he was ten minutes late to meet up with Tommy Wilhelm, so he rushed down the hall to his locker, took out his jacket and Redskins cap, and ran down the back stairs out onto the playground.

Douglas Baer was at the bottom of the steps leaning against the school building just above the playing fields, looking off into the middle distance.

"Have you seen Tommy?" Joshua asked.

Douglas pointed in the direction of the lower field.

"Playing soccer," Douglas said. "Most of the fourth-grade boys are down there."

"Are you coming?" Joshua asked.

"Tommy didn't ask me," Douglas said.

"Do you have to be invited to play soccer at recess?" Joshua said.

"That's the way it is in fourth grade," Douglas said. "Tommy Wilhelm's in charge."

"Why don't you come with me?" Joshua asked.

"No, thanks," Douglas said. "I hate Tommy Wilhelm."

Joshua shrugged. He knew exactly how Douglas felt. He remembered very well what it was like to be left out, and he still worried about it now, worried about it always.

He headed down the hill to the lower field where Tommy Wilhelm and a lot of the fourth-grade boys were playing soccer.

"Did you see Douglas?" Ethan asked, coming up behind Joshua.

"Yeah," Joshua said. "Up by the steps."

"Mad?" Ethan asked.

"He seemed sad," Joshua said.

"He's on Tommy's wrong side," Ethan said, hurrying down the hill with Joshua.

"How come?" Joshua said, although he certainly knew what it was like to be on Tommy Wilhelm's wrong side.

"Tommy's decided that Douglas is a nerd," Ethan said. "I don't know why. Douglas is my fourth best friend." He looked over at Joshua. "Actually, you're my fourth best friend and Douglas is my fifth."

And he ran onto the field, taking a place on Tommy Wilhelm's defense playing against the fifth grade.

Joshua waited. He didn't ask to play but stood on the sidelines hoping to be asked. Nothing happened. Tommy Wilhelm didn't even seem to notice him, although Ethan called out, "Joshua can play fullback." But Joshua wasn't asked to play fullback. So he stood on one foot and then the other, his hands in the pockets of his ski jacket, waiting for the bell to signal the end of recess.

Maybe Tommy had decided he was a nerd again. Maybe Tommy had already forgotten how cool he thought it was for Joshua to come to school with a cigarette behind his ear. Maybe he'd forgotten that after math class he'd asked Joshua to meet him on the lower field.

Joshua was beginning to feel the way he had when he was held back in third grade.

"Weak is how I feel," he'd told his mother.

If Andrew were there instead of at home sick, then things would be different. If he were there standing at the edge of the soccer field with Joshua, he would say, "So what?"

"If Tommy doesn't like me," Joshua would say, "nobody will."

"Don't worry so much about what Tommy thinks, Josh," Andrew would say. "He's a bully."

"That's what my mother says."

"Mine too," Andrew would say.

Joshua knew that Andrew worried, too. Once last year Tommy wrote CHICKEN in chalk on the back of Andrew's jacket without his knowing and all through math everybody in the third grade but Andrew knew and didn't tell him. Not even Joshua. That's how it was with Tommy Wilhelm in charge of the class.

That afternoon walking home together, Joshua's arm slung over Andrew's shoulder, commiserating with his best friend, Andrew had said, "I wish Tommy Wilhelm would disappear."

"Me too," Joshua said.

"At least I wish there was something we could do so he wasn't so powerful," Andrew had said.

"Like what?"

Andrew shrugged. "Like I don't know. Maybe ignore him."

"We could try that tomorrow," Joshua said.

But it was difficult to ignore Tommy Wilhelm.

When the bell rang, Joshua was the first up the hill, passing Mr. Regan and Douglas Baer talking at the bottom of the steps, rushing two stairs at a time to his locker.

"So did you get to play?" Douglas asked, coming up the corridor just as Joshua opened his locker.

"Nope," Joshua said.

"I didn't think you would," Douglas said.

With a familiar sense of failure, Joshua hung up his jacket, took out his book bag with his library book and notebook for writing compositions, and some M & M's that Amanda had given him that morning.

"I don't much like soccer anyway," Joshua said to Douglas, and headed down the corridor to homeroom, where English class was held.

ROBERT NEWTON PECK has written more than sixty books for adults and children, including the acclaimed *A Day No Pigs Would Die* and its sequel, *A Part of the Sky*. *Soup 1776* is the fourteenth installment in the popular Soup series. Among Mr. Peck's other titles are *Soup*, *Soup on Wheels*, *Soup for President*, and *Nine Man Tree* (Random House, 1998).

He lives in Longwood, Florida.

SOUP 1776

PRAISE FOR *SOUP 1776*:

"The action is fast-paced . . . and the play is a blast! Well-written and fun to read."

—*School Library Journal*

"Preteens will find the characters and mayhem hilarious."

—*Booklist*

"Clever and lively."

—*Childsplay*

from

Soup
1776

by Robert Newton Peck

Miss Kelly faced us all.

"Today," she said, "marks our final day of school."

Needless to say, we cheered.

Our teacher, eyeing the little bottle of Anacin on her desk, said, "*Everyone* in this room may look forward to a peaceful summer vacation."

Mumbles of approval swept through the room.

"In only a few more days," Miss Kelly went on to say, "we will celebrate the Fourth of July. As you know, our town is performing a pageant, in honor of Battle Victory Day. If we all pitch in, we can reward our friend Miss Boland with an event she shall forever cherish."

As she spoke, I was deeply involved in cherishing Norma Jean Bissell. Ah, the cherry of her cheek. Yet I was plagued by the problems of pageantry. Life, for me, wouldn't be a cherry.

It would be a pit.

Beside me, on our bench, perched like an expectant vulture, sat Luther Wesley Vinson.

Soup, I feared, had planned something to involve me, not in Disability's Disaster, but in my own. Last night, I couldn't sleep. Tossing and turning in bed, I kept worrying about what we'd collected at the dump. A chair cushion, a variety of belts, plus curtain rings, a dumbbell, and a blanket. Not to mention two eggbeaters. Nothing, I concluded, could assemble from so absurd an assortment. Not by anyone sane. But my pal was crazier than Crazy Horse.

Again, I was gazing at Norma Jean when Soup poked an elbow into my ribs.

"Rob," he whispered, "you won't believe what a heroic role we'll be playing in our pageant. And a certain young lady is going to be delirious at the derring of your do."

"What is it?" I asked in wild anticipation.

"There's only five of us," Soup said. "Yet, in our very own unassuming way, we shall rescue the entire town from, if I may employ a sorry term, Disability's Disaster."

"Five of us?"

Soup nodded. "A big five. Now, as soon as Miss Kelly decides to parole us, you and I, old tiger, have a cheerful chore to perform."

"What is it?" I asked, hoping I'd never know.

Soup grinned. "It's arts and crafts."

My day dragged. Miss Kelly lectured us all on history, and we had to study more about 1776, in *Hotbeds of History* by Dr. P. H. Dee. For some reason, Miss Kelly kept repeating his name.

Why? I couldn't begin to guess. Then, as I'd ignored all else, our teacher decided to spring her major announcement.

"I have important news," Miss Kelly said. "A person of renown is going to visit Learning on Battle Victory Day. Someone famous. His name is Dr. P. H. Dee, and he is a — "

"Wrestler," said Janice Riker.

Miss Kelly flinched. "No, he is a scholar. Dr. Dee is dedicated to supervising as many historical pageants as possible, at taxpayers' expense, to see that all amateur productions adhere to established data and are historically and politically correct."

"Trouble," hissed Soup.

I cringed.

"Rob, we've taken a few *liberties*, to use a Revolutionary term, in composing *your* script. This old Dr. P. H. Dee geezer might muddy our waters. We may have to take drastic action."

"Please," I begged. "Whatever you're thinking, do not think it."

Soup Vinson braced his spine. "Robert, my boy, there comes a moment in the life of every hero, a time to counterpunch correctness and allow the winners to win."

"Redcoats or patriots?"

Without answering, Soup slyly smiled.

School let out. We scholars, standing in line at the door, shook hands with Miss Kelly, thanking her for enduring one more year that had gouged another notch in her soul. At least it had nudged her twelve months closer to retirement and eternal rest.

"Home we go," I said.

"Later," said Soup. "First, we hightail it toward The Dump, there to put together our prize."

Minutes later, there we were, unloading all of the elements that we had assembled on the night when I was convinced I was still sleeping.

"Okay," said Soup. "Here's my blueprint."

Viewing our assortment of trash, I had no clue as to Soup's intention. Worse yet, I was reluctant to ask, as my fingers fondled one of our twin eggbeaters. I spun its little crank.

"Rob," said Soup, "begin by looping all of our belts together. Don't ask me how. Just do it."

I did it.

"The little dumbbell," Soup said, "belongs in front, like this, handle straight up. See? Now only one of its ends shows. You and I hold down the middle, behind it, on the cushion."

"Where do the belts go?"

"Underneath, to serve as straps. Insert a few of them into the curtain rings."

"Why?"

Soup stared at me. "Rob, please don't tell me that you don't savvy it. Not after you and I have sat through all those cowboy movies." Without further explanation, Soup finished securing the dumbbell at one of the short sides of the rectangular chair cushion. "There," he said. "That's our horn."

"You mean," I asked him, "like a Little Bighorn?"

"Sort of. Next we handle the belts. They'll meander around the cushion. I've never constructed one of these before, so suffer along with me, gallant soldier."

I suffered.

Nothing that my pal was saying, or doing, served even a smack of sense. Having no idea what we were making, or why we were making it, contributed to my concern.

"Soup," I said, "there's only one way to end all of this. You and I had better pack up and run away from home. As far as we can."

"Retreat?"

I nodded. "Yes, to escape jail."

Soup stood straighter. "Rob, a Wahooligan never retreats. A Wahooligan advances, dead ahead, to reap the rewards of realism in spite of the cowboy movies."

"I don't get it," I told Soup.

I didn't. Why, I kept wondering, did Soup persist in all this crazy cowboy chatter? It had nothing to do with 1776. Was this palaver a part of his pathetic procedure? I moaned. Had I been alive, I'd have cried.

To darken the day even worse, Dr. P. H. Dee was due to arrive in Learning to observe our local disaster. And, I fretted, to report all tamperings with the truth to the police. Soup and I would be arrested. I'd hang. And, after that, Papa and Mama would scold me forever.

"Why?" I asked Soup, while studying the mess we seemed to

be making. "Why do we have to be *inventors?*"

"To be famous," Soup said. "Maybe next year Miss Kelly will give us an exam. And I want you to be well informed. So, let's consider ourselves as the brothers who invented the airplane, Wilbur and Orville Redenbacher."

"Okay."

"Tie an eggbeater on your side of the cushion," Soup instructed, "while I attach the other one on mine. Each eggbeater has to hang blades up and handle down."

"Anything you say," I said, too weary to argue, yet wondering why we needed belts and eggbeaters on a chair. All this, plus the fact that the blanket smelled like a horse. A dead one.

"It looks perfect," Soup said.

"I hope this gizmo isn't for me. Is it?"

"Well, it's actual for both of us. You in front, and I in rear. Behind you." Soup giggled. "Behind the dumbbell."

"Soup, how come I always go first?"

"Because," he sighed, "you're a born leader. Now all we have to do is prepare the two costumes that you and I shall wear. That'll be easy because we won't be wearing much."

"We're going to be in a *costume?*"

"Of course," said Soup. "We're the stars. We upstage Chief Sitting Duck and Bold Beaver and Wet Blanket." He smirked. "One might say that we're the Last of the Wahooligans."

"Thank goodness. For a while, I was afraid you wanted us to be cowboys . . . on horseback."

"Wahooligans," said Soup, giving his eggbeater a testing tug, "never rode horses. Here," he pointed to our thing, "is what we shall ride astride."

"An old ripped chair cushion?"

"You're catching on. Rob, it's all working out in my mind. We arrive at the battle scene with a peace pipe. You and I restore order. Not only do we save the pageant, we heal the petty bickering. Without bloodshed."

"If we're a couple of Wahooligans," I asked Soup, "exactly who are we? What do we use for names?"

"Me . . . Spreadeagle. You . . . Lonely Skunk."

My teeth gritted. "You're saying that you get to play an eagle, and I have to be a *skunk*?"

Soup grinned. "As luck would have it."

"Darn you, Soup," I said, kicking the cushion. "I can't impress Norma Jean by riding a beat-up eggbeater and calling myself Lonely Skunk."

"This," said Soup, pointing at our constructed contraption, "is more than you think. We sit here, the dumbbell is our horn, and our feet hang down to stuff into the eggbeater handles for stirrups."

"It's a saddle? So we can ride a *horse*?"

"No," said Soup. "We ride a mule."

110

ANN CAMERON is the best-selling author of many popular books for children, including *The Stories Julian Tells*, *More Stories Julian Tells*, and *The Stories Huey Tells*. Her other books include *Julian, Dream Doctor*; *Julian, Secret Agent*; *Julian's Glorious Summer*; *The Most Beautiful Place in the World*; *The Kidnapped Prince*; and *The Secret Life of Amanda K. Woods* (Farrar, Straus and Giroux, 1998).

Ms. Cameron lives in Guatemala.

PRAISE FOR *MORE STORIES HUEY TELLS*:

"A realistic view of a child's world in language that emerging readers can easily grasp...expressive illustrations are certain to elicit smiles."

—*School Library Journal*

"Subtle, complicated, and profoundly moving...this is a book for sharing in the classroom and at home."

—*Booklist*

"A satisfying series for young independent readers."
—*The New York Times Book Review*

PRAISE FOR *THE STORIES HUEY TELLS*:

"A warm, friendly chapter book...Kids everywhere will recognize their fears, dreams, and jokes in Huey's daily adventures."

—*Booklist*

"A wonderful book...an irresistible hero."

—*The Boston Sunday Globe*

A Bulletin of the Center for Children's Books Blue Ribbon Book

from MORE STORIES HUEY TELLS

by ANN CAMERON

The Night I Turned Fifteen Billion

Dad was wearing the party hat we'd fixed for him. It was made out of white paper with lots of glitter glued on it. We had drawn two big A's on it with a blue marker, and all around them we'd painted gold stars and yellow comets and lots of colored spirals that my mom said were the shapes of some galaxies the stars are in.

We—my family, plus my dog, Spunky, and our friends Gloria, Shavaun, and Shavaun's brother, Tyrone—were having a party for Dad in our yard. He had just got an A in his first college course—an astronomy class. He took the class to learn about the universe. Besides, he told us, every minute he'd think about astronomy would be one less minute trying not to think about smoking cigarettes.

Astronomy is the study of the stars. That's why we put stars and comets and galaxies on Dad's hat. We were having the party at twilight, so later we could sit on the blankets we had spread out in the yard and watch the stars come out.

First we played a game we made up called meteor tag. If the person who was It tagged us before we got to the blankets, we were "out"—vaporized by the earth's atmosphere. If we got back to the blankets, we were meteors landed on Earth. When Dad was It, he chased us all over the yard, and we dived into the blankets just like meteors landing. If he hadn't slowed down to hold on to his party hat, and if Spunky hadn't run in front of him, he would have vaporized us every time.

After a while we got tired, and hungry, too. Then Gloria and Julian and I went into the kitchen for the star-shaped cookies and the special punch we'd made. "Milky Way Galactic Punch" is what we called it. We made it out of milk, because of the name of the galaxy Earth is in—the Milky Way. Julian put lots of shredded coconut in it to be star dust and comets and meteors. I put in lots of ice to be empty space, and butterscotch chips to be the stars.

I carried the biggest glass of all to my dad and explained what all the stuff in it was supposed to be. He swallowed some. "Very good!" he said. "Very chewy—but very galactic."

We all got in a circle around Dad, and Julian gave a toast in his honor. "To Dad, a student of the universe!" he said. We clinked glasses.

"Thank you," Dad said. "I wasn't sure I could learn so

much stuff—but I did it!" He lifted his special hat and bowed.

Above us, the sky was getting dark. I saw one star, and then I saw more and more—just like they were showing up for the party. The sky got velvety black. We lay on our backs on the blankets and used Gloria's binoculars to look at the stars.

"There are hundreds!" Shavaun said.

"Maybe more!" Gloria said.

I looked. "There are *lots*," I said.

I tried to show the stars to Spunky through the binoculars. Maybe he needed special dog binoculars, because he kept trying to look down at the grass.

"There are billions more stars than we can see," Dad said. "My professor said there are a thousand billion, just in our galaxy."

Shavaun shaded his eyes with his hands and stared upward. "How does he know?" he asked. "Seems like it could take a person's whole life to count to a thousand billion. No time out for lunch or holidays, no movies, no baseball games. Nothing. And then, suppose you got to be seven hundred years old, and you'd counted to five hundred billion, and your brother or somebody interrupted you and you had to start counting over? Even if you'd been friends 695 years, you'd want to break his head!"

"No astronomer's counted the stars one by one," Dad explained. "No human being could do it. What astronomers have done is count the stars in one little part of a galaxy. Then they estimate how much bigger a galaxy is than the little part where they counted, and how many galaxies there are, and how big the universe is. Then they do some multiplying. That's how they number the stars. They can't do it exactly. They just make their best guess."

We were silent, just flattening ourselves to the grass and looking up and up and up.

"Way, way up there somewhere there might be people," Gloria said.

"My professor said there are a billion trillion planets," Dad said. "Out of so many, some must be like Earth..."

"Way far from here," my mom said quietly, "right this minute, some creatures kind of like us are probably out in their yard having a party, looking across the universe and wondering if we exist."

"Why can't we see them? Why can't they see us?" I asked.

"We're too far apart," my dad said. "We don't know where they are. And they don't know where we are. But maybe some-day we'll all travel in spaceships, and far, far from our homes we'll meet."

"What started the universe?" Julian asked.

"That's hard to explain," my dad said. "The astronomers say it used to be small. In fact, tiny. Just one very tiny point. Then there was an explosion. It happened fifteen billion years ago. Something blew up. Something like—well, a kind of magic firecracker energy seed.

"Except—it wasn't really a thing. It existed before time and before space. Before anything. So they can't say when it was, or where, or what. They can't say why it blew up, or if some other being made it. That's why it's like magic.

"In one second, the magic firecracker energy seed made all the subatomic particles in the universe. Then the particles spent fifteen billion years spreading out and becoming stars and planets and plants and animals and people."

"So we all are really old when we're born," my mom said, wonderingly. "All the particles in our bodies are as old as the universe."

"That means we're all fifteen billion years old!" Tyrone said.

I couldn't believe it.

I'm not seven, I thought. I'm fifteen billion! I pinched myself all over, trying to feel the oldness in me. I pinched Spunky, and he yelped.

"What did you do to Spunky?" my mom said.

"I was just looking for his particles," I said.

Mom frowned. "Don't pinch Spunky just because everything is fifteen billion years old!"

"People don't know this," Julian said. "We should have a yard sale! We can sell everything as antique. We can advertise.

'Fifteen-billion-year-old family sells all!' A lot of people will come."

"They might!" my dad said. "Except we would have to tell them *everything* in the universe is fifteen billion years old. Then they might just decide the fifteen-billion-year-old stuff they already have is okay. They might just keep their fifteen-billion-year-old money and go home."

"Besides," my mom said, "I like our stuff even if it is old."

"I guess we don't need their antique money anyway," Julian said. But he sounded disappointed.

I thought of a riddle.

> *What's right here and far away?*
> *What's right now and long ago?*

I asked it.

"The universe," Gloria said.

"Right!" I said.

"It's here, and it's far away. It's old, and it's young," Dad agreed. "And everything in it is spinning and flying farther and farther out into space. Us, too."

Tyrone sat up. "If you were going to explore space, what would you take with you?" he asked.

"Universal money," Julian said.

"Pictures of back home," Shavaun said.

"Friends," Gloria said.

I patted Spunky. "A dog and a lot of dog food," I said.

"A suitcase full of memories," my mother said. "Because memories tell us who we've been and who we are. 'Cause if we aren't anybody, there's no use going anywhere."

"Myself, I'd take all my favorite songs," Tyrone said. "On the other side of the universe, I'd teach them to somebody."

"I'd take a time machine," my dad said, "so I could go back to all the best times and places."

"Stop by here!" my mom said. "Because there'll never be another night just like tonight."

"I'd come back to here," my dad said. "I won't forget tonight." Then he looked at his watch. "It's nine o'clock," he said. "Past the kids' bedtime."

"We shouldn't have a bedtime!" Julian protested. "We don't *need* a bedtime. We're fifteen billion years old!"

But my folks said it was our bedtime, all the same.

We carried our antique blankets and glasses in. Dad brought in his brand-new antique hat.

On the floor of our room, we fixed up sleeping bags for Gloria, Shavaun, and Tyrone.

My mom turned the lights out. She said that just this one time, as long as we were in bed, we could stay up talking till nine-thirty.

We didn't talk very much because we threw pillows instead. We pretended that they were universes colliding, and the feathers that came out were star dust. Like us.

When a whole bunch of feathers came out, Spunky barked.

My dad stuck his head in the door. He said nobody was supposed to be moving around.

We said nothing was moving around, just Spunky and the universe.

"For human children," my dad said, "it's time to sleep."

"Yes, sir," we said. We were quiet. In the dark, we tried finding the feathers that had come out of the pillows and sticking them back in. But that didn't work.

"We'll get them in the morning," Julian whispered.

It was a really special night. We never had so many friends sleep over before.

The universe is too big to be alone in, I thought. Probably even the stars are happy that they have each other.

I wondered how you knew *exactly* when the particles that made you became fifteen billion years old. I could say I turned fifteen billion the night I found out about them.

It seemed like I should feel some wisdom inside from my ancient particles—but when I tried to feel it, I couldn't.

I could just feel Spunky's chest expand as he breathed, and hear everybody else softly breathing.

The subatomic particles that make our bodies had zoomed around the universe for almost fifteen billion years before they became us. It seemed like a miracle that they finally *had* made us—that we were all in our house together, on Earth, under the sky, among the stars.

For a minute I imagined the universe and everything in it the way Dad said it was—all kind of loose and flying around like crazy. I hugged Spunky.

"Julian," I whispered, "are you *sure* we're really here?"

"Huh?" Julian said, half-asleep. And then he whispered, "Yes."

WENDELIN VAN DRAANEN is a computer science instructor, a wife, a mom, a runner of dogs, and a part-time singer in a rock band. She also rises at 5 a.m. each morning to write funny stories about smart, determined young women.

Sammy Keyes and the Hotel Thief will be available in hardcover from Knopf in Spring 1998, with a paperback edition to follow in Fall 1998. Ms. Van Draanen lives in Santa Maria, California, where she has just finished the next **Sammy Keyes** mystery, *Sammy Keyes and the Skeleton Man*, and is at work on another.

PRAISE FOR *SAMMY KEYES AND THE HOTEL THIEF*:

"If Kinsey Millhone ever hires a junior partner, Sammy Keyes will be the first candidate on the list. She's feisty, fearless, and funny. A top-notch investigator!"

—*Sue Grafton, author of* A Is for Alibi *through* M Is for Malice

"A great story with plenty of shivers and suspense. Make friends with Samantha Keyes."

—*Joan Lowery Nixon, current president of the Mystery Writers of America, four-time winner of the Edgar Award, and author of* The Other Side of Dark

"This girl sleuth is no well-mannered Nancy Drew. She's endearingly hot-tempered, nosy and not always obedient—in short, she's someone I want to read about again. A winning debut!"

—*Margaret Maron, author of* The Bootlegger's Daughter *(and other mysteries starring Judge Deborah Knott) and* One Coffee With *(and other mysteries starring Sigrid Harald)*

SAMMY KEYES AND THE HOTEL THIEF

from

sammy keyes
AND THE hotel thief

by Wendelin Van Draanen

I really thought it might only take a minute and that Grams wouldn't even notice I was late. I thought wrong. There were kids hanging around outside the Heavenly Hotel, peeking in the windows, but they didn't seem to know anything. And since the door was propped open, I just walked right in.

There were only adults inside, so I found a spot where I thought the policemen wouldn't notice me—right behind one of those Pope-hat chairs.

Now, I don't mind policemen. Actually, when I was in the fourth grade I wanted to *be* one, but that was before Lady Lana left me with Grams and I had to start worrying about someone finding out. When you're living where you're not supposed to be living it doesn't take long to figure out that you should stay away from people who ask nosy questions, and believe me, policemen like to ask *lots* of nosy questions.

And you could tell—they'd been asking this one lady lots and *lots* of nosy questions. The lady was wearing a dress that looked like it was made out of metal, tiny silver hoops all linked together that kind of shimmered when she moved. She had on pointy silver high heels and silver nylons, and she was yelling at the police at the top of her lungs.

Her head was shaking back and forth so much that these big silver balls on the ends of her earrings were swinging around, practically hitting her in the cheeks. She had really long finger-nails that were painted black with silver moons and stars, and her hair was all swirled around on top of her head and plastered with hair spray.

I moved a little bit closer, behind another Pope-hat chair. The policeman was telling her, "Now, miss, please, calm down."

"Quit telling me to calm down! I'll calm down when you find my money!"

Two policemen are there taking the report, but I can only see the face of the one. He's tall and skinny and has lots of white teeth and a stringy little mustache. He says, "You say it was four thousand dollars?"

"What are you, deaf? Yes, four thousand dollars!"

The policeman scribbles away in his notebook. "And why did you say you were carrying this much cash around?"

Those earrings start flying again. "I *didn't* say, and it's none of your business! Your business is to find out who stole it from me!"

Tall 'n' Skinny just scribbles some more in his notebook, then tugs on a corner of his mustache and says, "We'll do our best."

She throws her hands up in the air. "That's *it*? That's all you're gonna do? What about fingerprints? Aren't you at least going to look for fingerprints?"

And before I can stop myself, I step out from behind the Pope-hat chair and say, "You won't find any fingerprints."

For a second, everything's quiet. Tall 'n' Skinny quits playing with his mustache, and the lady's earrings come in for a landing. Then everyone—and I mean *everyone*—turns around and stares at me. All of a sudden my throat's feeling kind of ticklish, so it only comes out as a whisper when I say, "He was wearing gloves."

The second policeman turns around to look at me, and I just want to disappear.

It's Officer Borsch, the man behind my one and only experience with the law. See, he gave me a ticket once. For jaywalking. And it's not like it's so bad, getting a ticket for jaywalking, it's just that I thought it was *stupid*. So I gave him the wrong name. The wrong name, and the wrong everything else.

So there I am, staring at him, trying like mad to remember the name I gave him when I got caught jaywalking. And I'm thinking that maybe I *shouldn't* remember it, because he's staring at me like he's trying to remember who I am, and if I give him the name I made up maybe he *will* remember, and then I'll be in some major trouble, when the lady croaks out, "*What* did you say?"

I mumble, "He was wearing gloves."

Officer Borsch says, "*Who* was wearing gloves?"

I try to shrink a few inches. "The man I saw on the fourth floor taking money out of a purse."

The lady yells, "See!"

Officer Borsch squints at me. "And how did you happen to see someone on the fourth floor stealing money out of a purse?"

Now you have to understand, Officer Borsch isn't the kind of man it's easy to lie to. He's big. He's Mikey, all grown up and in a very bad mood. His hair's done with Crisco, and his shirt is so tight it looks like he's trying to press it from the inside out. On top of that he's nosy. Very nosy. When he gave me that ticket for jaywalking he must've asked me a hundred questions that didn't have a thing to do with jaywalking. And I thought I was so smart, answering every single one of them with a lie. I remember throwing the ticket away in a Dumpster, feeling like I'd just hit a home run, and now here I was—face to face with the Borsch-man, on the verge of getting thrown into Juvenile Hall.

"I asked you a question!"

"Huh? Oh! Ummmmmm..." I look around and can tell—everyone knows I'm trying to think up a lie. So I blurt out, "I saw him through binoculars."

"Binoculars?" he says. "From where?"

I try to sound real calm. "From across the street."

Officer Borsch squints even harder. "You want to tell me

you could see someone clear up on the fourth floor from across the street?"

I nod and he blows air out of his mouth like a deflating balloon.

"Leave her alone!" The lady moves in a little closer to me. "Go ahead, honey, tell me what you saw."

I look at her for a minute, thinking that four thousand dollars is an awful lot of money and that if it were mine I sure would want it back. Finally I say, "I was visiting my grandmother in the Senior Highrise. I was bored, so I started looking around with the binoculars and I saw some guy taking money out of a purse."

She grabs me by the shoulders and I can feel her little fingernail galaxies digging into my back. "When? *When* did you see this?"

"About an hour ago."

She yells at Tall 'n' Skinny, "What did I tell you?" then turns back to me. "And honey, what did this man look like?"

"He had brown hair and a brown beard, and he was wearing black gloves and a black jacket."

Officer Borsch pushes the lady aside. "Was he tall, was he short?"

"Kind of medium."

"What kind of jacket was it?"

"It was straight with big pockets."

"What do you mean, 'straight'?" he asks.

"You know—it wasn't puffy, it was straight."

"Heavy?"

"Kind of medium."

He shakes his head. "'Kind of medium'—oh that's a *real* good description."

Well, let me tell you, I didn't like the way he was rolling his eyes and talking down to me. He was treating me like a stupid little kid, and I'm *not* a stupid little kid. So when he sighs and says, "Could you at least tell me, was he skinny or fat?" I point to Tall 'n' Skinny and say, "Well, he wasn't as skinny as him..." then I point to the Borsch-man, "...and he sure wasn't as fat as you."

The lady just busts up, but Officer Borsch doesn't think it's too funny. His neck gets kind of red and he puts his face right next to mine. "Look, little girl, we've had five burglaries in this vicinity in the past two weeks. We don't have time for your wisecracks. If you know something, tell us. If you don't, or if you're just making all this up, then go home to your mommy and let us do our work."

The lady steps in. "Honey, how old do you think he was?"

Well, I'm okay at guessing some things, but age is not one of them. "I don't know, maybe...forty?"

Officer Borsch mumbles, "Kind of medium, huh?" and then laughs like he's the funniest guy in the building. He clears his throat. "Look, we'll get your name and number and if we have any further questions we'll just call you."

There goes my heart again, knocking away in my chest. "I've told you everything I can think of." *Except*, I'm thinking, *the fact that it feels like I've seen this guy somewhere before.*

Tall 'n' Skinny flips open his notebook. "Well just in case, let's get your name and address."

Great. And I'm thinking, *How do I get myself into these things?* when out of my mouth pops, "Samantha Keyes, 6375 East Jasmine."

Now, if they were thinking at all they would've taken one look at me and known—there's no way I live on East Jasmine. East Jasmine is where they have two houses to a block. East Jasmine is where they have gates in front of their driveways and riding mowers for their lawns. East Jasmine is where people from out of town go just to gawk.

And 6375 East Jasmine is where Marissa lives.

Tall 'n' Skinny doesn't even blink. He just scribbles it down and says, "Very good. We'll contact you if we need you."

So I say to the lady, "I hope you get your money back," and then head out the door.

One of the kids outside calls, "Hey, what's going on in there?"

I shrug, "Just a burglary." And I'm about to jaywalk across the street when I glance back at the Heavenly and see Officer Borsch watching me through the doorway.

I stop and head down to the intersection, because I can tell—Officer Borsch is not going to sleep well until he remembers just exactly where he's run into me before.

Knopf Paperbacks are available wherever books are sold.

KAREN ACKERMAN

THE NIGHT CROSSING
ISBN 0-679-87040-7
$4.50 U.S. / $6.00 CAN.

JENNIFER ARMSTRONG

**BLACK-EYED
SUSAN**
ISBN 0-679-88556-0
$4.99 U.S. / $6.50 CAN.

**MARY MEHAN
AWAKE**
Paperback available
Fall 1998
ISBN 0-679-89265-6
$4.99 U.S. / $6.50 CAN.

**THE DREAMS OF
MAIRHE MEHAN**
ISBN 0-679-88557-9
$4.99 U.S. / $6.50 CAN.

AVI

NO MORE MAGIC
ISBN 0-394-85001-7
$4.99 U.S. / $6.50 CAN.

**WHO STOLE THE
WIZARD OF OZ?**
ISBN 0-394-84992-2
$4.99 / $6.50 CAN.

ESTHER WOOD ——— ROBIN F. BRANCATO
BRADY

TOLIVER'S SECRET
ISBN 0-679-84804-5
$4.99 U.S. / $6.50 CAN.

WINNING
ISBN 0-394-80751-0
$4.99 U.S. / $6.50 CAN.

ANN CAMERON ———————————

**THE STORIES
JULIAN TELLS**
ISBN 0-394-82892-5
$4.99 U.S. / $6.50 CAN.

**MORE STORIES
JULIAN TELLS**
ISBN 0-394-82454-7
$4.99 U.S. / $6.50 CAN.

**MORE STORIES
HUEY TELLS**
*Paperback available
Winter 1998*
ISBN 0-679-88363-0
$4.99 U.S. / $6.50 CAN.

**THE STORIES
HUEY TELLS**
ISBN 0-679-88559-5
$4.99 U.S. / $6.50 CAN.

**THE MOST
BEAUTIFUL PLACE
IN THE WORLD**
ISBN 0-394-80424-4
$3.99 U.S. / $5.50 CAN.

DEBORAH DAVIS

**THE SECRET OF
THE SEAL**
ISBN 0-679-86566-7
$3.99 U.S. / $5.50 CAN.

MONICA FURLONG

JUNIPER
ISBN 0-679-83369-2
$4.99 U.S. / $6.50 CAN.

WISE CHILD
ISBN 0-394-82598-5
$4.99 U.S. / $6.50 CAN.

**ROBIN'S
COUNTRY**
ISBN 0-679-89099-8
$4.99 U.S.

VIRGINIA
HAMILTON

**ANTHONY BURNS:
THE DEFEAT AND
TRIUMPH OF A
FUGITIVE SLAVE**
ISBN 0-679-83997-6
$4.99 U.S. / $6.50 CAN.

RUSSELL HOBAN —— MAVIS JUKES ——

THE TROKEVILLE WAY
ISBN 0-679-88560-9
$4.99 U.S.

BLACKBERRIES IN THE DARK
SBN 0-679-86570-5
$3.99 U.S. / $5.50 CAN.

DICK KING-SMITH ———————————

BABE: THE GALLANT PIG
ISBN 0-679-87393-7
$4.99 U.S.

HARRY'S MAD
ISBN 0-679-88688-5
$4.99 U.S

ACE: THE VERY IMPORTANT PIG
ISBN 0-679-81931-2
$4.99 U.S.

MARTIN'S MICE
ISBN 0-679-89098-X
$4.99 U.S.

DICK KING-SMITH *(cont.)*

THE INVISIBLE DOG
ISBN 0-679-87041-5
$4.99 U.S.

THREE TERRIBLE TRINS
ISBN 0-679-88552-8
$4.99 U.S.

HARRIET'S HARE
ISBN 0-679-88551-X
$4.99 U.S.

THE STRAY
ISBN 0-679-89101-3
$4.99 U.S.

PAUL MANY

THESE ARE THE RULES
ISBN 0-679-88978-7
$4.99 U.S. / $6.50 CAN.

BETTY MILES

THE SECRET LIFE OF THE UNDERWEAR CHAMP
ISBN 0-394-84563-3
$4.99 U.S. / $6.50 CAN.

ROBERT NEWTON PECK

SOUP
Paperback available Fall 1998
ISBN 0-679-89261-3
$4.99 U.S. / $6.50 CAN.

SOUP FOR PRESIDENT
Paperback available Fall 1998
ISBN 0-679-89259-1
$4.99 U.S. / $6.50 CAN.

SOUP ON WHEELS
Paperback available Fall 1998
ISBN 0-679-89260-5
$4.99 U.S. / $6.50 CAN.

SOUP AHOY
ISBN 0-679-87617-0
$4.50 U.S. / $6.00 CAN.

SOUP 1776
Paperback available Fall 1998
ISBN 0-679-89262-1
$4.99 U.S. / $6.50 CAN.

PHILIP PULLMAN

THE GOLDEN COMPASS
Paperback available
Fall 1998
ISBN 0-679-87924-2
$8.99 U.S. / $11.50 CAN.

THE RUBY IN THE SMOKE
ISBN 0-394-89589-4
$4.99 U.S.

SHADOW IN THE NORTH
ISBN 0-394-82599-3
$4.99 U.S.

THE TIGER IN THE WELL
ISBN 0-679-82671-8
$4.99 U.S.

PHILLIP PULLMAN (cont.)

THE TIN PRINCESS
ISBN 0-679-87615-4
$4.99 U.S.

THE BROKEN BRIDGE
ISBN 0-679-84715-4
$4.99 U.S. / $6.50 CAN.

THE WHITE MERCEDES
ISBN 0-679-88623-0
$4.99 U.S. / $6.50 CAN.

LOUIS SACHAR

THERE'S A BOY IN THE GIRLS' BATHROOM
ISBN 0-394-80572-0
$4.99 U.S. / $6.50 CAN.

THE BOY WHO LOST HIS FACE
ISBN 0-679-80160-X
$4.99 U.S. / $6.50 CAN.

DOGS DON'T TELL JOKES
ISBN 0-679-83372-2
$4.99 U.S. / $6.50 CAN.

SUSAN SHREVE

**THE FLUNKING OF
JOSHUA T. BATES**
ISBN 0-679-84187-3
$4.99 U.S. / $6.50 CAN.

**JOSHUA T. BATES
TAKES CHARGE**
ISBN 0-679-87039-3
$4.99 U.S. / $6.50 CAN.

**JOSHUA T. BATES IN
TROUBLE AGAIN**
Paperback available Fall 1998
ISBN 0-679-89263-X
$4.99 U.S. / $6.50 CAN.

ETHEL FOOTMAN SMOTHERS —— JERRY SPINELLI——

**DOWN IN THE
PINEY WOODS**
ISBN 0-679-84714-6
$3.99 U.S. / $4.99 CAN

CRASH
ISBN 0-679-88550-1
$4.99 U.S. / $6.50 CAN.

SUZANNE FISHER STAPLES

SHABANU
ISBN 0-679-81030-7
$4.99 U.S. / $6.50 CAN.

HAVELI
ISBN 0-679-86569-1
$4.99 U.S. / $6.50 CAN.

MARY STOLZ

CEZANNE PINTO
ISBN 0-679-88933-7
$4.99 U.S. / $6.50 CAN.

ERIKA TAMAR

THE JUNKYARD DO
ISBN 0-679-88561-7
$4.99 U.S. / $6.50 CAN.

WENDELIN VAN DRAANEN

SAMMY KEYES AND THE HOTEL THIEF
Paperback available Fall 1998
ISBN 0-679-89264-8
$4.99 U.S. / $6.50 CAN.

RICH WALLACE

SHOTS ON GOAL
Paperback available Fall 1998
ISBN 0-679-88671-0
$4.99 U.S. / $6.50 CAN.

WRESTLING STURBRIDGE
ISBN 0-679-88555-2
$4.99 U.S. / $6.50 CAN.

MILDRED PITTS WALTER

**JUSTIN AND THE BEST
BISCUITS IN THE WORLD**
ISBN 0-679-80346-7
$3.99 U.S. / $5.50 CAN.

SALLY WARNER

DOG YEARS
ISBN 0-679-88553-6
$4.99 U.S. / $6.50 CAN.

SOME FRIEND
ISBN 0-679-87619-7
$4.99 U.S. / $6.50 CAN.

ELLIE & THE BUNHEADS
ISBN 0-679-89097-1
$4.99 U.S. / $6.50 CAN.

GLORIA WHELAN —— ELVIRA WOODRUFF

GOODBYE, VIETNAM
ISBN 0-679-82376-X
$3.99 U.S. / $5.50 CAN.

DEAR LEVI: LETTERS FROM THE OVERLAND TRAIL
ISBN 0-679-88558-7
$4.99 U.S. / $6.50 CAN.

KNOPF PAPERBACKS
A Fiction Sampler
Books for Young Readers
201 East 50th Street, MD 30-2 • New York, NY 10022

Copyright © 1998 by Alfred A. Knopf

All contents and prices in this sampler are subject to change without notice